HONOR EMPOWERED

Guardians of the Fae Realms: Book 12
JL Madore

Honor Empowered: Guardians of the Fae Realms

JL Madore -- 1st ed.

ISBN: 978-1-998372-69-0

CHAPTER ONE

Honor

$\mathcal{I}$ am Honor Thornebane, Princess of Dornte, Guardian of the Crown, and mate to Lukas, Tundra, Dune, and Shadow. To the citizens of the Fae Realm, the Dornte quadrant, and the people within the castle, I'm a symbol of leadership and protection. Not only a royal, I'm the one who heads up our quadrant's elite fighting force—the Amberloq Warriors.

I am much more than that—at least to my mates.

And thank the stars for that.

When the five of us are alone in our suite, the veneers of our public personas are removed. Lukas isn't the Director of Operations for the Fae Concealment office. Tundra and Dune aren't the Amberloq Biome Guardians for the Snowy Peaks or Desert Plains. And Shadow isn't a late-onset Fae Oracle with no training on how to handle that.

No. When we're naked and keyed up and getting our horizontal hijinks fix, we are just us.

Growing up, I knew the possibility existed I could be matched with three Amberloq Biome Guardians to ensure the safety of the quadrant. My predecessor, my aunt, Princess Valorous, chose not to take that path.

The result was disastrous.

I push away thoughts of politics and the devastation of past mistakes and stay in the moment.

My point is, within the suite for the Guardian of the Crown, we are simply five people who have come together in a symbiotic, polyamorous mating.

Our home in Amberloq Hall is designed specifically for that purpose, and everything is supersized to take that into account. That suits us very well indeed because with two of my mates having seven-foot, head-to-toe wingspans, we need space in both our bed and our shower.

The five-person shower in our suite boasts adjustable jet sprayers—which Dune is currently playing with to hit all my erogenous zones—an angled bench on the back wall—where Shadow is currently bent over Lukas's lap sucking him off—and a few rubberized kneeling mats. Tundra is currently getting those in place at my feet, preparing for his advance.

Reaching over my head, Dune secures my wrists into the ceiling grips, and slides in behind me. I test the hold, my position ensuring the water from the overhead nozzles slides down my curves in warm streams.

Water cascading down bare flesh is hella sexy.

Tundra lifts my right leg and hooks it over his broad shoulder. When his mouth fuses on my core, I groan and grind against his ministration.

Tundra loves oral. No complaints here.

I arch back giving him the best possible access to my core. The fervent swipe of his tongue is glorious and since Dune has been ruthlessly teasing and toying with me, I need some targeted attention.

"Oh, yes! That. Thank you, T."

Dune chuckles next to my ear. "Is our boy taking advantage of my prep work? That hardly seems fair."

"Looks like you'll just have to find another playground, sandman."

"With pleasure." Dune reaches to the wall dispenser and gives the nozzle a couple of pumps.

After a few shower adventures, Dune decided that aside from the dispenser with the shampoo, conditioner, and body wash, we needed a second one that he filled with lube.

"Any playground preferences?" Dune asks, eyeing me up and down as if inventorying his options.

"Consider me your territory to claim. Plant your flag, warrior." I know where he's headed before he slicks his fingers over the entrance to my ass.

Dune is an anal whore. He likes to play, fuck, and be fucked. There's nothing taboo to him. And if he's getting the green light, you can bet that's where he's headed. "Slecking hell, your ass is so sweet."

His fingers massage the crack of my ass as he presses up behind me, his cock hard against my flesh. A rush of cream warms my pussy and Tundra growls lapping and suckling and swallowing it down.

A zing of sensation hits me and the water falling from the showerhead makes my nipples peak even more. "Oh, you boys. So good."

Tundra slides two, long fingers inside me, and my internal muscles grip and pulse around him. At the same time, Lukas grunts over on the bench. His head is back, his jaw clenched, and the throaty panting of his release is an almost Pavlovian trigger to ramp me up.

I watch our mage come undone, his chest rising and falling in panting breaths as Shadow's head bobs over his cock.

Shadow is blind but he has incredible tactile skills.

Damn. With both Dune and Tundra fingering me, Tundra

working me over with his mouth, and watching Lukas and Shadow, I'm not going to last long.

I groan as the pressure of my arousal builds and I pant, hauling in the humid air of our shower paradise.

I'm lost to them.

Pulling against the wrist cuffs, I arc my body and grind against my guys. If they were anyone else, I'm sure I'd be mortified.

They aren't. These are my mates.

Dune reaches around me from behind, his free hand caressing over the wet mound of my breast before he pinches my nipple.

The pressure isn't gentlemanly and the sweet agony triggers my release to detonate.

I cry out as my body shatters. The quakes of pleasure rack me, and as good as it is... "I need more. Fuck, I need to be filled."

Dune nips my ear and chuckles. "As you wish."

The loss of his and Tundra's fingers leave me empty inside, but they will take care of that in short order. In the next moment, the water is turned off, Tundra releases my wrists, and I'm wrapped in a mile of plush towel to be carried to our bed.

Or at least, I thought we were headed for the bed.

Instead, Dune takes me to the large, square ottoman bench in front of couches by our fireplace. He lays me down, opens the towel, and spreads it out so I'm bare to the room. The loss of the heat from the warm water and then the towel makes me shiver.

Tundra watches my nipples tighten and swallows. "Don't worry, Princess. We're about to heat you up."

Dune grins and signals for me to roll over onto my stomach. "Assume the position, beautiful."

I do as I'm asked.

Tundra kneels at my head and with gentle hands, sweeps my hair off my shoulders.

The drizzle of massage oil starts at the nape of my neck and drips a cool trail all the way to my ass crack.

Another shiver racks me but this one has nothing to do with being chilly. "You know, boys, it defeats the purpose of showering if you slather me in oil and sex."

"Not if we shower again after," Dune says, waggling his sandy blond brows at me.

"And then we're caught in a vicious cycle." I groan as he caresses over my spinal ridges and rubs the spot where my wings break free.

"Always so responsive," Dune says, increasing the pressure as his fingers glide up and down the erogenous zone. "I bet I could make you come hard just by rubbing you off along these sexy ridges."

"Been there, done that," Lukas says, joining us with Shadow. He leads our elven counselor over to join us and settles him on his knees on the floor. Bending him over the spread-out towel covering the ottoman, he pops open the lid of a bottle of lube. "It's an orgasm definitely worth revisiting."

I fold my hands under my cheeks and turn my head to smile at him. "You know where I live."

His gaze is heated and hungry. "That I do."

Tundra moves to stand behind Dune, where my feet hang off the massive, tufted square. While Dune massages his way down my lower back, nearing his end goal, Tundra takes the massage oil and starts addressing the massage of my feet.

Ohmygod, I love my feet rubbed.

I'd close my eyes if it wouldn't rob me from watching Lukas lining up to penetrate Shadow. Reaching to the side, I claim Shadow's hand and squeeze. "Looks like we're the lucky two on the receiving end for the moment, eh sweetie?"

Shadow closes his eyes and exhales as Lukas does his thing, prepping for entry. His body isn't thickly muscled like Dune and Tundra's or military fit like Lukas's. Shadow's elven genes make him a slender male with elegant, graceful lines, and a beauty to die for.

Sweet mercies, I love my life.

Dune

Slecking hell, I love my life. Glancing down, I watch my cock glisten with anticipation as I finish prepping Honor. Obsessed. I think I might be clinically obsessed with taking her ass. There's something so wrong and yet so incredibly right about it.

And she loves it.

It wouldn't hold any appeal if it didn't send her pheromones through the ceiling. But it does.

Finishing her massage, I'm happy to say our princess is as relaxed as ever. I grab the bottle of lubrication Shadow brought to the event and squirt a healthy dose into my palm. Gripping my cock, I glide my hand from base to tip and then take the excess and swipe it right where I'm headed.

Our princess is resting on her belly watching Lukas do unto Shadow what I intend to do to her. Climbing up onto the flat, cushioned plain, I hook my arm under her belly and bring her up onto her knees. "Am I still free to plant my flag?"

"Yes, please."

That's my girl. With all the foreplay taken care of, I line the swollen head of my cock up with the pinched muscles of her backside and penetrate her slow and steady. It's such exquisite torture knowing what's coming and yet giving her the time to adjust.

Not that it takes long. Honor is a greedy girl and is soon groaning and pumping her hips to urge me on. It doesn't take much urging.

"Slecking hell, you're so deliciously tight."

Her feminine pleasure scents the air and I grip her hips, watching my cock glisten as it glides in and out of her. I could live and die doing this for the rest of my life and be happy... except I'm not the only one waiting to get inside of her.

Tundra is the strong and silent warrior of our quint but that doesn't mean he's not communicating his needs with me right now. One look at the heated storm brewing in those eyes of his and there's no mistaking it.

"Fine, Iceman. You're up."

Urging Honor to stretch out on her belly, I lower myself with her and then roll us onto our backs. Now I'm on the bottom, she's facing the ceiling on top of me and I'm still snuggly nestled inside her.

"Open your legs for me," Tundra says, his voice graveled and deep.

I swallow and meet his heated gaze as Honor and I make room for him between our legs. Tundra is a big guy and needs room for those muscled thighs. He drops onto all fours and lines up with her core. There's no need for a preamble.

She's wet and hungry and getting aggressive about needing someone sexing her.

"Any requests?" he asks, bending forward to claim her mouth.

"Fill me," she breathes. "I want both of you hard and fucking me."

Her words trigger a wild pressure at the base of my cock, and I fight not to go off early.

No. This is just getting good.

Tundra may be a totally uptight and by-the-book guardian, but all his pent-up energy comes out in sex. He's a machine. He's also damned talented.

"As you wish, my love. Brace yourself."

I feel the tightening of Honor's insides as he penetrates her and fills her pussy. Reaching under her arms, I hug her to my chest and play with her nipples.

The beauty of being the bottom bread in this sexy sandwich is I can lay here, feel everything, and watch Tundra's expression as well as Lukas and Shadow's.

It's the best.

It doesn't take our Snowy Peaks representative long before he's building up a solid rhythm and is hitting home. The ottoman rocks gently with each thrust, but thankfully the floor of the bedroom is carpeted and this ottoman is a solid block of furniture.

If we were on legs poised over hardwood or tiles, we'd be scraping our way across the room.

Did I mention Tundra is a machine?

"Oh...!" Honor gasps, arching her chest as her breath escapes.

Oh damn. I groan as the rise of her ribs has her grinding down on my cock and the shift in position allows me to feel the thrust and retreat of Tundra's cock even more keenly.

It's as if he's rubbing right against me.

Honor's muscles are steadily tightening, greedy for her building release to take hold.

I close my eyes to block out how hot Tundra is when he's hammering into her...or into me...or, well, into anyone I suppose.

It's all so ball-achingly good.

"You grip me so hard when he's inside you," Tundra says.

"You're welcome," I say, my voice thready.

"Harder, T," Honor gasps, the tremors of her release taking hold. "Don't hold back on me."

The slap of flesh-on-flesh—both from the three of us and from Lukas and Shadow going hard at it—is loud and fills the suite.

Honor's body starts to quiver, and her throaty feminine

gasps signal the beginning of her next orgasm. I tighten my grip around her ribs and flex my hips, penetrating deeper while Tundra does his thing.

The first couple of times we were together like this, I worried we would be too much for her—but when she's wound up and hungry, our Princess can take everything we give her.

"That's it, baby," I gasp, dizzy with the pleasure coming at me from all sides. "Feel him rub your insides and lose your mind."

Shadow stiffens beside us, and Lukas slams his hips forward. The throaty grunt he lets off as he locks in place is all about the power of blowing his load.

Watching them go off is too much.

I'm already on a cliff and hanging by a thread and...

Honor's core pulses and grabs hold. Tundra's punishing pace sends her careening over the cliff with me.

She shatters and I'm lost.

As her body stiffens, she clenches and squeezes my cock so good, I swear I might die from the pleasure.

Tundra slows down a little to give us time to ride out our orgasms. Honor convulses in my arms, and I give her everything I have.

When our hearts start to beat again, Tundra gets back to business. It doesn't take him long after that. He hammers home for a few more wild minutes, then his wings snap open above us, and his hips start to kick.

His face contorts with the ecstasy of losing himself inside our female. He's too much.

Having been lovers with him for the past two years, it's a pleasure to watch as he spills into our mate and to know how far we've come. Back then we were enemy fuck buddies. Now we're mates.

Tundra's expression eases from the tortured pleasure of his release to the exquisite reverence of admiring our princess.

She tugs his mouth to hers and claims his mouth. "Thanks,

iceman." Then she turns her head to the side and twists to kiss me. "That was lovely, boys."

I close my eyes and try to remember how to breathe.

Here with my mates, our bodies saturated in the mixed scents of sweat, orgasms, and our passion for one another, I can't help but feel like I gamed the system and ended up the winner of a lottery I never deserved to enter. Doesn't matter...

It's mine now and I'll never give it up.

CHAPTER TWO

Lukas

*A*s much as I'd love for the five of us to spend all our days and nights naked and isolated in Amberloq Hall, sadly that's not realistic. We've still got to track down Ruic Breard, wipe out the rebellion, build up the Amberloq, figure out Shadow's oracle powers, and decipher what the end of his prophecy means.

The good news is, we're in good shape as a quint.

With the budding relationships taking hold and deepening into something meaningful, we're falling into step with one another as teammates.

Even with everything coming at us, I'm hopeful we have a real chance to get this right.

"Good morning." Demarco shuffles into the kitchen and scans the counter. "Oh, thank the gods, you made coffee.

I chuckle and point to the cupboard he needs to find himself a mug. People who look at him see an elderly man with short blond hair and a trimmed beard. What they don't see is just how elderly he is.

Although, as draconians go, seven hundred isn't that old. Unlike Rhylan, Demarco's dragon race doesn't shift into a dragon beast, he simply has the strength, wisdom, and longevity of his ancestry.

And a few parlor tricks.

Demarco pours himself a mug full of java, sticks his finger in it to adjust the temperature using his gifts, and takes a long swallow. "Ambrosia. Any chance the big man with the white wings is cooking this morning? That stew he made the other night was incredible."

I chuckle. Demarco has always been driven by his passion to consume food, alcohol, and women.

"Tundra was showered and getting dressed when I came down. I'm sure he'll be along shortly."

"Excellent. Considering he and the other winged one don't wear shirts, getting dressed shouldn't take long." He takes another long sip and comes to sit with me at the table. "I admit, it's odd seeing you sitting here, relaxed, and not rushing out to be Hawk Barron's sidekick."

I lean back in my chair and smile. "There have been a lot of changes over the past year. Hawk has four warrior mates who watch his back for him now. He doesn't need me."

He arches a skeptical brow. "I'm sure that's not true. You were more than his guard dog. You were the man who helped him keep all the balls in the air."

"Yeah, well, Brant and Jaxx help him with that now and if he needs me, he knows where I am."

He glances around at the massive kitchen and chuckles. "You're one of five people living in a lodge built for hundreds. This place is eerily empty."

I shrug. "I don't know. We kind of like having it to ourselves."

He takes another drink of his coffee and laughs. "Fewer ears to hear the throes of orgasm coming from your suite."

Now it's my turn to laugh. "I have our suite spelled for silence. You're only guessing."

"Five to a bed? It's not so much of a guess as a fond reflection of my own experiences. I was once young too, you know."

"Who are you trying to kid? You were probably getting on with four others last week."

His grin tells me I'm right. "Sadly, my escapades will have to be put on hold for a few months while I sort things out here with you lot."

I sober and make sure he can read my sincerity. "I can't thank you enough for coming and agreeing to help Shadow. He's an incredible man and him suffering through this without you would destroy us."

"We can't have that. And since you seem to have the space to put me up, I'm happy to offer my assistance. Who is supposed to live here, anyway?"

"The Amberloq Warriors," Tundra says, stepping in to join us. "Sorry for the interruption. Is it all right if I get started on breakfast?"

"More than all right." My senses fire to life as I take in my mate. Tundra is a tall, strong male, and seeing him in designer jeans, bare-chested, and fresh from the shower is a pleasure. "Demarco was asking about the possibility of your culinary skills filling his belly."

Tundra gives our guest a nod and sets two large frying pans onto the stovetop. "I was thinking of making a granosh if that suits you. The brownies keep our refrigerator stocked, so we have everything I need."

I sit back and sip from the edge of my mug. "I have no idea what that is, Iceman, but you've never let us down. Go for it."

Demarco shrugs. "I never argue with the cook. Whatever you're inspired to create is good with me."

With that, Tundra pulls a stack of fresh ingredients out of

the fridge, a couple of bowls from the cupboard, and gets to work washing and chopping.

"So, tell me more about the Amberloq Warriors," Demarco says, moving across the table so he doesn't have his back to Tundra. "Judging by the number of bedrooms here, I assume there's an army of them."

"Until two years ago that was true," Tundra says washing a couple of tomatoes, a bunch of cilantro, and some colorful mushrooms. "Almost all of our force was slaughtered by a witch. It was only last week when we discovered a small group of survivors being held prisoner deep in the Badlands."

"An exciting time for the Amberloq."

"It is."

"How many were found?"

"Not enough," I say, sitting back in my chair. "The warriors of the Amberloq have stood as those who guard the crown of Dornte. Sadly, when the reign of the last Thornebane king was usurped, almost all of that force was lost."

"So, it's regroup and rebuild time, I assume," Demarco says.

"Sharp as always, my friend. Yes, Honor is responsible for re-establishing the warrior force for the quadrant. At the same time, we have to bring down the rebels still trying to undermine Creed's rule."

"And Creed is Honor's brother?"

I nod. "And now brother-in-law to both me and Hawk through our mates."

Demarco chuckles. "One big happy royal family."

"We are," Honor says, arriving arm-in-arm with Shadow.

The two of them have damp hair, relaxed smiles, and by the spring in Shadow's step, I wouldn't be surprised if our princess honored our elven lover with a little private attention before coming down.

Which is not only distractingly sexy and firing my imagination to life, but also lovely. Shadow has had a rough month and deserves a little TLC…a lot, really.

Honor escorts Shadow to us and when she unhooks his hand from her arm, she sets it on the edge of the table so he can find his seat and settle in. "The fourteen of us are a mad jumble of skills, lovers, siblings, and friends, but it works."

"It seems to," Demarco says. "Between all of you racing around putting out fires, there doesn't seem to be much time for anything else but family and mates."

"Which is fine by us," Honor says. "Although, with Calli and her guys back in the Human Realm, I admit, I wish we had a bit more free time. I'd like to be able to spare a day trip or two. I don't want my little godson to forget who I am."

"Impossible, babe." I meet her gaze and wink. "You are utterly unforgettable."

The aroma of sizzling mushrooms, onions, and cooking oils is getting stronger in the air and makes my stomach growl. I get up to stretch my legs and go over to check out breakfast in progress.

"Damn, T, this smells amazing." I lean over the stove to get a lungful. "I wasn't that hungry before but now that I'm breathing this in, I'm ravenous."

He sends me a sinful smile and leans in close to lower his voice. "I'm not surprised you need to refuel. You worked up an appetite this morning with Shadow. Any chance you've got anything left in you? Maybe a kiss the cook session?"

The heated look he gives me shoots straight to my groin. I glance down at the front of my jeans and frown. "Look what you did. We're in a room with our guest and I'm throwing wood."

Tundra chuckles and then curses and spins back to stir. "And I almost burned the vegetables. Off you go, troublemaker. A chef's got to concentrate."

"Troublemaker? You started it."

Tundra laughs. "I suppose that's true."

I step in front of him, so his back and wings are screening Demarco from what I'm doing. After a quick unzip, I secure his wrist, and slide his hand down the front of my pants.

My cock pulses against his palm and I grind into his hold. Claiming his mouth, I groan and kiss him with every ounce of hunger I have for him. I wish we had time to satiate this pull we share, but the sizzling of mixed veggies says we don't.

Pulling back, I'm pleased I'm not the only one breathless. "That kiss the cook moment is just a taste. Now I'm not alone in my suffering. First chance we get, we're naked and riding rough."

Tundra strokes me a couple of times and my knees nearly buckle. "Let me get breakfast served and then I'm all yours."

I step back and ease out of his grip. "It's a plan."

"Are you boys burning our breakfast?" Honor hollers from the other side of the kitchen.

"Shit," Tundra hisses, rushing to stir the cut veggies frying in the pan. "No, it's fine. Just lost focus there for a moment, Princess. All is well. Nothing to see here."

Shadow

I chuckle at the lie as Tundra turns back to the stove, hastily reclaims his spoon, and stirs. At the same time, Lukas adjusts the lay of things inside his pants, and Honor and Demarco go back to chatting.

No one else could've seen what was happening but Moonshade came in from walking the perimeter with Dune and sat right beside the stove, looking up at the chef and hoping for scraps.

Our vision link is growing stronger every day and so is our

partnership bond. Even in the short time I've had her with me, we've grown to love and trust one another. She is such a good little wolf.

Especially when she lets me see moments like that.

Part of me feels guilty for Lukas's hunger for Tundra. Our mage has been focusing on me and my needs to keep me from panicking during the tailspin spiral of my life.

It's sweet but unnecessary.

What is meant to happen will happen and he doesn't have the power to stop it. There are other people who need to connect in this mating fivesome.

Like me and Honor, for instance.

Having her mouth sucking me to orgasm before we came down was perfection. A stolen moment meant to be nothing more than a declaration of mutual love and attraction.

"Come, sweeting," I say, calling my little wolf from being a voyeur. Her nails click on the hard stone floor, and I see a flash of realization on Lukas's face as he realizes where she was sitting.

"Why are you grinning like that, counselor?" Dune asks, taking the seat next to me.

I lean down, pick up Moonshade when she arrives, and settle her in my lap. "It's just illuminating to see the world through my sweet girl's eyes."

Lukas slides quickly back into his seat and covers his lap with a napkin. "We could use her as a little undercover spy."

"We could. She's very stealthy," I say, fighting back my amusement. "People don't even realize she's there taking it all in."

Lukas chuckles to himself, reclaims his coffee mug, and raises it to me in a private toast.

"What did I miss?" Dune asks, looking from Lukas to me and back again.

"Nothing worth repeating in front of our house guest," Lukas says sobering. "And we are eternally grateful for you being here, Demarco. And for you helping Shadow when you first arrived. And for you agreeing to stay on for the foreseeable future to continue helping."

Demarco shares a knowing look with Lukas and shrugs. "To say that I owe you my life doesn't even begin to cover it. It does my heart good to begin to settle my debt to you."

Lukas waves that away. "I've told you for years, there is no debt owed."

"And I've told you for years, that's horseshit."

Tundra picks that moment to bring over two platters of an egg and veggie hash with thin pancake things that smell like heaven. "This is a traditional breakfast in the peaks. I hope you enjoy it."

"You eat it like a taco." Dune grabs a stack of clean plates off the sideboard and hands them out. "Having eaten it a hundred times during the Mount Hekko years, I can honestly say, you are in for a treat."

"Excellent. I look forward to it," Demarco says, waiting until Honor gets her portions before beginning. "Eat up Shadow. You and I have a long day ahead of us. And Princess, if you're available, I'd like to claim some of your time as well."

Honor pauses with her fork at her mouth. "Of course. Anything you need."

"In that case, if your brother and his doctor mate are available, perhaps they could join us as well."

CHAPTER THREE

Tundra

Dune and I leave Lukas and Honor to work with Shadow and fly over to the castle. The two of us haven't had a lot of time alone since this mating adventure began and it's nice to spend a few peaceful moments flying together like old times.

Well, in truth, there were no peaceful moments with Dune in the old times.

Still, it's nice to spend time with him, just the two of us sharing the air. "Do you mind if we circle over the entire perimeter of the royal grounds?" I ask, not wanting to end the moment so soon.

"Sure. What are you thinking? Rebels? Security weak spots?"

I hear the alarm in his voice and feel guilty for putting it there. "Only that it's nice to be alone with you like this. I want more of it."

The strain of his momentary worry eases, and his expression softens. "Are you becoming a romantic, Iceman? That sounded dangerously close to a loving compliment."

"I've always been a romantic. You simply didn't bring it out in me before now."

He chuckles. "I brought other things out in you."

"True. Hostility, frustration, exhaustion."

"Passion, hunger, dominance."

We're both right. In the two years we were exiled together, I would get frustrated and angry with him, and my alpha warrior side would rear its head and then I'd want to dominate him. "It may not have been the healthiest outlet, but the two of us had some wild and sexually explosive moments."

"It's almost a shame those times are over."

I shake my head. "No. If you want me to dominate you, I'd much rather do it with a passionate love pumping in my veins."

"As long as something is pumping hard, I'm in."

I swallow, my groin tightening with the prospect. "Both the Phoenix Quint and Creed's quad have sexual playrooms. Maybe we need to look into getting some equipment."

Dune's gaze widens as a sultry smile spreads across his face. "Do tell. When did you find this out? And how come I know nothing about it?"

I roll my eyes. "My point wasn't to gossip about the others but to point out that with a multiple lover situation like ours, having other sexual outlets might be fun."

"Agreed. Let's make that happen. We can use one of the spare rooms in our suite." Dune swings his wings in the air, so he swoops onto his back. "I volunteer to be tied up first."

My laughter flows so easily with him now I can hardly believe we're the same two people we've been for years. "Let's keep our minds on the trouble at hand. We've got rebels to squash, a mint to open, and a force of warriors to ready."

Dune rubs his fingers over his nipples and bites his lip. "But you'd rather be pounding into me, right?"

The fact that he's flying upside down is as ridiculous as he is. "No question. Still, we are warriors, not animals. We have self-control and can pick and choose when to act on our desires as the situation deems appropriate."

Dune flips back to fly normally and laughs. "Always the mature one. Fine. I will play the part of a Biome General for the outside world but deep down, I will be imagining myself trussed and tied and you getting down and dirty with me."

I try to laugh his words off, but it's a half-hearted attempt at best. Now that he's planted the image, it's imperative that we make that happen.

Dune

Iceman is laughing off my interest in his Dom idea, but I can tell how jacked up he is at the prospect. He's also right about knowing where and when to make that happen. We're about to meet with Creed and Rhylan about quadrant business and need to focus.

The two of us land at the northern entrance of the castle and the guards open the double doors to let us pass. Once inside I grip his wrist and shove him against the wall.

"A quick kiss isn't what my body is aching for at all, but as you said, we have to be adults and respect our duty. Later, however, we're going to revisit this idea of yours."

His hand slides up my battle vest and around my back, pulling me closer. "I look forward to it."

I take my kiss and step back. "See how mature I can be?"

"The transformation is incredible," he jokes, tugging me into motion. "I can barely recognize the man you've become."

I let him have that one. I'm still me. I'll always be me...and he'll always be rigid and too serious for his own good.

The two of us walk through the castle, place our hands on the ID screens at the doors to the lower level, and then take the stairs down into the basement. The security office is at the end of the corridor to the right.

"Do you think Demarco will be able to help Shadow?"

"Lukas thinks so, and I hope he's right."

"Yeah, me too. Shadow's a quiet guy, but he's smart and he always seems to get me."

"He's a skilled counselor. That likely gives him more insight into the things you do than most people can understand."

I crane my neck to the side to gawk at him. "Are you saying that only a therapist could understand me?"

Tundra lifts his shoulders looking unabashed. "Not only a therapist. Maybe a person like Shadow, as well as someone who takes the time to love you."

I casually brush the back of his hand with my fingers. "There you go getting romantic on me again."

~

Honor

Lukas occupies Moonshade for the morning and keeps an eye on Shadow. Since Demarco has several exercises and probing evaluations to work through before he'll be ready for me, Lukas suggests I use the time in the Guardian's Library going through the discs of stored knowledge from my predecessors.

Fine with me.

As much as I'd love to sit and watch Shadow work through his trials so I can help him later, the entire quadrant of Dornte is counting on me to get up to speed on my position and how to run the Amberloq.

And, as much as I appreciate the knowledge handed down, the Guardian Discs I'm most interested in are the ones Aunt Valorous may or may not have left for me at the other warrior hall.

If she was the leader I hope she was, she's left me wisdom to follow from beyond the grave. If she wasn't, then I'll have to make do with the information the others left.

I glance around the small rectangular room and press the next disc into the reader. When the lesson appears on the screen in front of my desk, I'm relieved it's not another disc describing the strategic advantage of high ground or the importance of weapon care.

I know each one is important in its own way, but there's only so much history and theory I can take before I start nodding off.

"Welcome, Guardian," the woman on the screen says. "Today I thought I would share a bit of recent history regarding the Garden District and the years-long wars between the witches, the nixies, the incubi, and the centaurs."

I check the timeframe of this disc based on its position on the shelves and figure this was about a hundred years ago. I don't think we even have incubi in the Garden District now. They populate most of the River Run.

Settling in, I grab my pen and search my desk for my notebook. *Damn.* I took it upstairs the other day to review my studies and must've forgotten to bring it back down.

"Hold that thought." Removing the disc, I set it next to the reader and rise to leave. Leaning over, I blow out the vanilla-scented candle and head for the vault door. "I'll be back to hear about the wars. Don't start without me."

I jump when I come face-to-face with Lukas on the other side of the door. He has his knuckles up to knock and drops the hand to pat his heart. "Sorry. I was coming to...Who were you talking to?"

"My great-great-great auntie someone. She was just about to tell me about a four fae war that raged on in the Garden District, but my notebook is upstairs."

He steps back and gives me room to pass and pull the vault door closed behind me. Having had raiders both here and at

Valorous's Hall try to break into the Guardian's Library, I'm very careful to keep it secure at all times.

There's no telling when someone might storm into the front foyer and make a grab for the Chronicle Discs.

"Did you need something, magic man?"

"I do. You."

I waggle my brows. "I like the sound of that, but we're supposed to be working."

"Funny girl. No. Demarco is ready for you now. If you're free to join him, I thought I'd take a break and check in with my teams."

"Of course. Those discs have been there for centuries. They can wait." I take his hand and the two of us exit the library and strike off toward the exercise room. "How are things going?"

"So far, so good. Demarco has tested how much the onset of the oracle powers has altered his brainwave patterns and motor functions. He thinks we're in fairly good shape and considering he's only had two or three episodes, he's optimistic."

I squeeze his hand. "Oh good. That's exactly the kind of news I was hoping for."

The doorbell chimes as we're walking through the house. My brother lets himself in and Doc follows.

Lukas and I change course to greet them.

"Thanks for coming," Lukas says.

I give my brother a hug. We're about the same height, but he's much broader and more muscled. He also smells like Doc's aftershave. "Where's Keyla?"

"I escorted her to the Portal Gate this morning. She's spending a few days with Calli, Kotah, and baby Ashborn."

I draw a deep breath. "I'm so jealous. I barely got a chance to hold the little guy and then he was gone."

"Yeah, they were anxious to get him back to the Human Realm to announce his birth and introduce him to Jaxx's family."

"And are they staying in the Pennsylvania Palace?"

Doc nods. "In the quint's private residence on the property, yeah. You gotta give Hawk props. When that man wants something built, he gets results."

"Speaking of getting results," Creed says, "I hear we've been invited to help Shadow with his oracle issues?"

"You have," Demarco says, entering the grand foyer. "It's a pleasure to meet you, King Creed, and you as well, doctor. I am Demarco of Dragon's Peak here to lend what aid I can. If you would, please follow me."

When we arrive at the exercise room, we find Shadow lying on his back with headphones over his pointed ears. His eyes are closed, his body is relaxed, and he looks like he might be seconds away from falling asleep.

Moonshade is curled up and sound asleep in the corner.

"That's weird," I say, pointing at our little wolf. "People came in the front door and now into this room and she hasn't woken up. She's usually much more of a guard wolf than that."

Demarco sends me a guilty smile. "That's my doing. I need Shadow to remain free of stimulus, so I spelled his little wolf asleep for the time being."

I'm not sure what he sees on my face, but he raises his palm.

"There's no need to stress. She's simply having a nap and will wake refreshed and with no ill effects."

"Oh, that's a relief."

"How is he doing?" Doc asks, studying Shadow across the room.

"Very well, considering. Mind you, we are in the early stages of his transition taking hold."

"Well, whatever we can do to help, consider it done," Creed says.

Demarco dips his chin. "Very good. The list of what Shadow will need is short but important. A few pieces of equipment, some medicinal homeopathy, and some touch-healing techniques I am hopeful you and your sister can help with. Honor mentioned your Mind Guardian gifts are a great deal stronger than hers."

Creed frowns at me, but I wave away his concern. "It's a fact. There's no sense glossing over it. You've always been stronger than I have."

Creed shakes his head and his long, silver hair sways freely around his shoulders. "Honor is mistaken. In our current state of training, I have more focus and strength but only because over the past two years I did little else but flex my mind, trying to kill the bitch queen who kept me prisoner. Honor is being self-deprecating. She underestimates her own strengths."

"He's being kind," I say.

Demarco shakes his head. "Either way, to have both of you solves any argument over the matter. Come, I will give you an anatomy lesson on how the energy patterns in an oracle's mind work differently than others, and then we'll discuss what you can do to help Shadow."

CHAPTER FOUR

Tundra

*D*une and I step into the security office of Thornebane Castle and find Rhylan standing at the war table sorting through data. "Knock knock."

The dragon looks up and waves us in. "Good morning, what can I do for you boys?"

"Actually, it's what we can do for you," Dune says. "We wanted to follow up on the progress of the mint sites. The last time we spoke about it, Creed was putting together a team with a liaison member from each of the quadrants and they were going to visit the potential sites. Where are we on that?"

Rhylan swipes his fingers across the screen of his tablet and images of the Central Mint appear. "It's been decided that the Central Mint is the location with the most power, the least political entanglement, and the closest to being production-ready. Creed plans to go out there today or tomorrow to meet the leaders of the other quadrants to get things started."

"We would like to attend that meeting as military support," Dune says.

Rhy nods. "I have no objection as long as you're the kind of support that is seen and not heard. I've caught wind of a few comments made regarding Dornte's weakness and how it's not up to the other three quadrants to bail us out of our civil unrest."

"That's bullshit," Dune grunts.

Rhylan arches a brow. "Of course, it is, but it will be Creed who addresses anything like that, not you two. He's fighting the stigma of being the lackey of his enemy for two years. We must project a strong and united front."

"We will," I assure him. "We won't cause him any political judgment."

"Good. I'll add you to the security roster."

I step over to read the intel on several of the men being displayed. "There are a couple of new faces here. Do you believe these are colluders with Breard and the goblin rebellion?"

"Possibly. All we know for certain is that we've scoured the quadrant from the badlands to the center of the city and we've come up empty. Ruic Breard has gone into hiding and someone with means is covering for him."

"Well, we took out his weapons cache and his illegal portal gate," Dune says. "That had to be a blow to his rebellion."

"I'm sure it was, but until we cut the head off the snake, there's no way to be sure it's over."

"What about the rebels who tried to take the castle?" I ask. "We injected them with trackers so we could keep an eye on their activities and locate them if we needed to."

Rhylan swipes across the screen again. "True. And other than these three, no one has stepped out of line."

"And these three?" Dune asks, searching the faces of the three. "How do we know they're up to something?"

"When we released them from our detainment after the castle was attacked, we asked each one of them to give us their place of employment and the address of their home. They were told that to go anywhere outside of those two places would trigger their trackers and notify us they were getting creative."

"And where have these three gone?"

He points to the first person in the array. "Linc Farrett was the easiest to find. When he veered from his approved route, I tracked his transport to an emergency call to the hospital. It seems Linc was the victim of a mugging on the way home from work and was taken for medical care."

"We can hardly fault him for that," I say.

"Of course not. I sent a man to the hospital just in case, but he was told to simply observe Mr. Farrett and let him know we'd be watching until he resumed his approved activities."

"And the other two?" Dune asks.

"The other two are a bit more of a mystery. Doric Spinlei either got tired of having a tracker and cut it out or someone who knew he had a tracker did it for him. Either way, we've recovered the tracker in a pool of a fair bit of blood but no Mr. Spinlei."

"Does he have a family?"

"He does and if we're to believe his wife, our rebel wannabe is a devoted family man who would never break his word to us and go missing. She insists he's fallen into a dangerous crowd, and something has happened to him."

"Poor Mr. Spinlei," I say with no sympathy at all. "He chose to ally himself with ruthless thugs and look at that, they weren't trustworthy."

"Funny how that works," Dune says, chuckling. He points to the third face in the photo array. "And lucky number three?"

"This is Bertru Cork, one of the few females who were involved in the castle raid. She went offline yesterday morning and just disappeared. No tracker to find. No sign of her at work or home. No family despite her listing two children and a dog."

I look closer at the picture. "Are you sure that's a female?"

Rhylan nods. "She's not much to look at, I know, but who

knows, maybe that has something to do with her life choices. In goblin society, females don't amount to much if they can't catch the eye of a male."

"Goblins suck," Dune says.

"No argument. Still, wherever Ms. Cork is, she's completely off the grid and we have no way of tracking her down."

I stare at the three faces. "This is interesting, but it doesn't offer us any insight into our current situation."

"No. You're right."

"Do you think it's possible to program a kill switch into the chips?" Dune asks. "You know so that if the bulk of them congregate and try something on a mass scale we take them out all at once?"

Rhylan blinks at Dune and then at me. "I don't think so. First, I don't think it's ethical to reprogram the chip since we already told them it was just for tracking and ensuring their whereabouts. Second, Creed isn't the kind of leader that will go for mass murder of his citizens—even if they are goblins."

"I'm not saying we kill them! What the hell gave you that idea, dragon? That's dark."

Rhylan makes a face at Dune. "You called it a kill switch and asked about taking them out."

"Oh, yeah. I see how you got there. My bad. No. I only meant drop them, not kill them."

"I'll give it some thought. For now, we're left working on the currency issue and—"

"Hold that thought," Dune says, scowling at one of the intake monitors on the wall. "Ruic Breard is live broadcasting as we speak."

"Pull it up to the war table hologram," I say.

Rhylan is already doing that and a moment later Ruic Breard, Dornte millionaire, and leader of the goblin rebellion is taking up our air space. "—with little regard to the people of Dornte and their wishes. I have tried to reason with the

Thornebane children but as young as they are, they don't yet see the wisdom of my offer."

"Here it comes," Rhylan says, rushing to his computer screen and calling up a banking safety net program we've been perfecting for weeks. "Come on, asshole, just get it over with."

"And so, it is with a heavy heart I must slap the wrist of these naughty children to teach them a lesson. As of right now, the Dornte banking system is frozen. I cannot in good conscience allow your hard-won savings to be left in the control of such a volatile rule. I apologize to my beloved citizens for the inconvenience, but it's something that must be done."

"Tundra, I'm downloading a backup file now. Go to the economic file and ensure it's updating. The file name is Leprechaun."

I jog over to the computer he's pointing to and call up the Leprechaun file. It's a massive data transfer, but the progress bar is filling in quickly. "It's here and the data cache looks good."

Rhylan claps his hands together and points at the image of the grinning goblin. "Got you motherfucker."

Then he pulls out his phone and hits a pre-programmed number. "Did you see Breard's announcement? Excellent. Cut his feed and run Creed's response."

As we watch, the grinning goblin is removed, and a pre-recorded message replaces it. "Citizens of Dornte. I apologize for the rantings of Mr. Breard and for any anxiety his scare tactics may have caused you. Understanding what kind of man he is, my cabinet has been working for weeks to not only secure your finances but to remove Breard Industries from our economic process altogether. I am proud to say we have come up with an incredibly stable and innovative solution."

"I bet Ruic Breard is about to lose his mind," Dune says chuckling.

Rhylan is on the phone again. "Chancellor Kaytee, this is Rhylan, King Creed's castle security officer and mate. We just issued the announcement of the safety measures. If you're in agreement that the Central Mint is our location, I'd like to get started right away. Yes, Chancellor."

He takes his call to the other room, and I return my attention to Creed and his recorded message. "We have taken minute-to-minute financial backups to ensure there will be little to no discrepancy to your accounts. We anticipated Breard Industries would try to hold the quadrant hostage through our finances since they haven't managed to do it physically. Yet again, Ruic and his followers have overestimated their power and underestimated ours. We, the people of Dornte, will stand strong."

Rhylan returns to the main security office sliding his arms into a leather jacket. "Okay, boys, you two head to the Stone-Haven Central Mint. Secure it and let me know if you spot any goblin activity. I don't anticipate Breard will be smart enough to figure it all out immediately but take no chances. I'll gather Creed and the others and meet you there."

I raise my eyebrows at Dune and smile at the light in his stunning turquoise eyes. "Meet you there."

Lukas

I feel helpless. Demarco is teaching Doc how to respond to the cortical spikes oracles suffer after prophesying, he's teaching Creed and Honor how to focus their natural psychic gifts to alleviate the stresses on his brain, and I'm in charge of entertaining Moonshade.

Don't get me wrong, I love our little wolf, but as a man accustomed to tracking down and tackling any foe that poses a threat to me or someone I care about, babysitting is hard.

I hear the roar of one of our side-by-side ATV buggies

outside and get up to go see who has come to visit. "Who do you think it is, baby girl?"

Moonshade bounces along beside me, her nails clicking on the floor as we go.

I wonder if Shadow is able to shut off the vision she's experiencing or if he's being flooded by the Blair Witch jumble of images. Demarco said he's going to teach him to access and turn off that connection going forward.

The two of us are almost to the entrance when Rhylan knocks and walks in. I can tell just by looking at him that something important is going on. "What's happened?"

"Breard just shut down the economy."

I grin and wave him to follow me. "And did our systems in place work?"

"Like a charm. Creed's going to be so jazzed."

The three of us arrive in the exercise room and Creed is already on his feet and coming to join us. "I'm going to be jazzed about what?"

Rhylan repeats his comment about Ruic Breard shutting down the economy in an attempt to lock us up and have the citizens turn against us.

"And we turned the tables?" Creed asked.

Rhy nods. "I activated the Leprechaun file the moment his people shut down his system and Tundra verified the backup is running. Chancellor Kaytee has been notified and is meeting us at the Central Mint as soon as we can get there."

"Hot damn," he says, straightening. He turns back to Demarco and Shadow and sobers. "I'm sorry to have to cut out early."

Demarco waves that away. "This isn't a one-day training. I'll be here for the next few months. Go, run your quadrant and we'll continue when you get back."

I go to Shadow and set my hands on his hips. "Are you okay if we leave you with Demarco?"

"Absolutely," he says. "Go, kick goblin ass."

"Hells yes," Honor says rushing over to give Shadow a quick kiss. "Love you, sweetie. We'll be back as soon as possible."

"We'll be fine."

"I'll hang here too," Doc says. "I want to have a solid understanding of what we'll be dealing with."

I clutch palms with Doc and give him a nod. "Much appreciated."

"Call us if you need us," Honor says, waving over her head as she jogs into the corridor and toward the front entrance.

The two of us grab our belongings from the front closet, have our jackets on, and are out the door a moment later.

And with that, Creed, Honor, Rhylan, and I climb into the side-by-side and head toward the castle motor pool.

"Damn, I wish we could've seen Breard's face when he realized he'd been outsmarted," Creed says.

I laugh. "Or when his techs tell him that he's now locked out of the quadrant's banking system."

Creed laughs. "Maybe we should send him a thank you card. After all, we never could've taken control if he hadn't shut things down on his end to give us the opening."

"That was brilliant strategic enlightenment," Rhylan says, shaking his head. "The fact that you and Hawk saw that coming and realized it was an opportunity instead of a guillotine hanging over our necks was slecking brilliant."

Honor squeezes my hand and I wink at her. "I'm glad it worked out. Hawk and I have had over a decade of dealing with self-important world leaders and tyrants. Almost all of them act in the same fashion. Once you start recognizing their patterns, you learn to predict their moves."

Honor releases the roll bar and grabs her silver hair, stopping it from lashing her in the face. "You're just being modest. Rhylan's right. It was a brilliant counter to their strongarming.

Now they're locked out and the joint currency production and distribution system is underway. It's revolutionary."

I love their enthusiasm, but there's still a lot to work out. "And hopefully it'll work. Don't forget, the hardest part of this plan is still ahead of you. Four government leaders from rival quadrants have to agree enough and work together enough to keep this project afloat."

Rhylan launches us over the rim of a grassy berm, and we bounce wildly onto the pavement where we park Hawk's SUVs.

Creed laughs and gives his dragon lover a look. "Can we arrive in StoneHaven without broken bones and whiplash, please?"

Rhylan shrugs. "Sorry, I'm excited and these machines are wicked fun."

Creed looks back at me and rolls his eyes. "What I was going to say is that I appreciate your cautionary approach. I understand there are hurdles to overcome but locking Breard Industries out on their ass is such sweet victory, we're just going to roll around in our gloating glee for a moment."

I laugh at his analogy, climbing out of the buggy and clicking the key fob to switch vehicles. "I get it. Roll away."

CHAPTER FIVE

Dune

$\mathcal{T}$undra and I arrive at the Central Mint in StoneHaven within half an hour. Before we land, the two of us make a security sweep of the area and check to ensure we're the first to arrive.

We are.

When we land on the front walk, I take my tablet out and scroll through my contacts. Tapping my selection, I hold the screen up and wait until the cute brunette appears on the screen. "Ensley, hey. I'm outside and the quadrant liaisons are on their way. Can you please come let me in?"

Ensley—formerly known as Mint Girl—grants me a wide smile. "So, this is real? When you called and asked me about the mint last week, I figured you were up to your old tricks and lying to get your kicks. Especially when you wouldn't tell me why you needed to know the things you were asking about."

"I wasn't lying. I simply wasn't at liberty to discuss what was happening yet."

"But now you can?"

36

"I could…if you let me in."

"How exciting. On my way."

I end the call and slide my tablet back into the thigh pocket of my tactical pants. A moment later, she pushes open the front door of the mint and I start to head in.

"If you two are all right, I'll wait out here," Tundra says, studying Ensley with a curious gaze. "The Chancellor is on her way and if the goblins figure out our site plans, it can't hurt to be watchful until things are locked in and underway."

"Sound logic, Iceman. I'll check on things inside." I leave him guarding the front door and with his hands clasped behind his back and his wings at attention, he's an imposing and impressive sight.

He's also slecking hot.

Ensley waves me through the museum at the front of the building. "When Chancellor Kaytee came through here with the leaders of the quadrant last week, she said they were simply visiting historical sites, but I could tell she was lying."

"It's hard to lie to a fae with your gifts."

"And yet, it's astonishing how often people do."

I glance around at the interior of the building. I suppose, being a protected site and a museum, I shouldn't be surprised that nothing has changed since I was last here. "Chancellor Kaytee is on her way to meet with King Creed. I'm not sure if the quadrant liaisons will all come, but there's a good chance."

"I knew it. We were just watching the video release from the Dornte king. Are *we* the stable and innovative solution he mentioned?"

I nod. "I proposed the Central Mint because I remembered how well-preserved and ready for production it was from the times we spent here. The council agreed and here we are."

Her eyes widen. "Really? *You* proposed it? You have the ear of King Creed?"

"I do. A lot happened in Dornte in the past three years and even more recently."

"I know. The whole Queen Laryssa rebellion was a mess and then King Creed and his sister reclaimed their realm. I don't follow the politics of the other quadrants closely, but I was happy for them. To have their parents killed like that was awful."

"It was."

"Is that how you know King Creed? Were the Amberloq finally able to rescue him? Is that what happened?"

"It was the Phoenix Quint and Creed's mates who reclaimed the throne. I got involved after that. I am bonded to Princess Honor. I am the Desert Plains Biome General."

Ensley busts up laughing and the musical tone bounces off the polished marble walls. "Bonded to the princess. That's hilarious. Yeah, Dune. I'm very sure."

I straighten and wait for her amusement to wind down. "I was just as skeptical while it was happening, but I assure you, now that things have settled, I'm very much committed to my mating and our quadrant."

She stops giggling and takes a closer look at me. "You're serious."

"I am. When Honor awoke from her confinement, the universe called me to duty and bound us as mates. It was a life-altering moment. I'm not the same male I was when you and I used to hook up."

Her expression morphs from utter amusement to amazement. "What a topsy-turvy world we live in."

I'm not surprised she found it hard to believe, but I'm getting tired of having to explain my personal life to her. "How many staff did it take to run the presses when the mint was in full production?"

She seems to recognize the change in subject and snaps back to her museum curator mode. "For set up and getting the presses running, seventeen. Once the production has begun, half of those would move into quality check, cutting, and counting."

"Is there a guild of workers or some kind of union for the tradesmen who work in mints?"

"Of course."

"How do we go about getting staffed?"

"I can get you the numbers of the people you'll need to contact. You'll also need to broker a contract for new plates, paper, ink, holographic technology, chemicals, and a few other things."

"I'll need an exhaustive list. Anything you can think of."

She swallows. "I'll get right on it. When are you thinking King Creed will want to begin production?"

I check the time on my watch and smile. "It's almost lunch now, so I don't want to be unreasonable. How about this afternoon?"

Honor

Lukas pulls the conveyance into a visitor's slot in front of the Central Mint. When the car is parked, he gestures for me to key in the necessary actions on the navigation panel.

"It's not as difficult as you make it out to be," I say, chuckling at him. "And for a man who basically ran security for the entire fae world in the Human Realm, I'm boggled by the block you put up on this."

Lukas shrugs. "Cars and trucks are machines to be utilized. They shouldn't ask questions or offer opinions when you need to go somewhere. They are a tool to get you from point A to point B and that is all. This AI hive mind network thing your world has going on with your cars is unnatural."

I bust up and program the car to wait indefinitely as we'll

need it to travel back to the StoneHaven Portal Hub. "Be careful what you call a tool to be utilized. Everyone knows that one day AI will take over the world."

"That's my point. Keep things simple. Sure, electronics in vehicles is good for heated seats and a navigation map, but that's where it should end."

Creed leans forward from the back seat and looks from Lukas to me. "Any chance we're wrapping up this titillating debate, so we can go inside and twist the knife on the goblin rebellion?"

"Yep. Sorry." I'm still chuckling when I get out and shut my door. "It's just fun for me to find something that Lukas doesn't adapt to and become the master of the moment he encounters."

My brother grins. "I can relate. Keyla is more gifted at adapt and conquer than anyone I've ever known."

"Present company excepted," Rhylan says, making a face at him.

Creed laughs. "Oh, of course. You're the man, Rhy. Sorry, I didn't mean to bruise your fragile ego."

Now it's Rhylan's turn to laugh. "I'm just slecking with you. Keyla is a marvel, no argument."

The four of us leave the parking lot and walk together up the steps of the building and toward Tundra standing tall at the front entrance.

"Hey, good looking. Any issues?" I say.

"No. None," Tundra says. "We arrived ten minutes ago and Dune went inside to get things started up with the Mint Girl he told us about."

"What's that now? What's he starting up with her? Should I be worried?"

Tundra shakes his head. "That came out wrong. He went inside to begin to assess the state of things with the female. His account of her being incredibly astute at her job seems to be accurate."

Funny-not funny. Even knowing Dune is on track with our mating bonds, a part of me reared up hearing Tundra's comment.

"I've never considered myself an overly possessive female-- Calli was dominating enough for both of us--but when you said that, I was ready to get violent."

"It's the bonding taking hold," Creed says. "It was the same with us."

"It's one of the reasons I was added into the royal mating," Rhylan says.

Creed nods. "I was obsessed and possessive. Even though I wanted to kick his ass, Keyla could see that it stemmed from a deep-rooted possession. I couldn't fight it. He was mine."

"He *is* yours," Rhylan corrects, winking at him. "And, on that note, your dragon lover must remind his king we are here on business. We need to get inside."

"Right you are, dragon. Let's see where we are and what we need to do to get rid of the goblin rebels once and for all."

"Yes please," I say, raising my knuckles to the door. "And good riddance."

"Let me get that for you, babe," Lukas says, passing his palm over the latch plate of the door and opening it using his gift.

I'm about to lead the group inside when a private car with tinted windows pulls to a stop at the end of the walkway. A man in a black suit with a rope-like tail gets out of the driver's seat and hurries behind the vehicle to open the back door from the other side.

Chancellor Kaytee is known throughout the four quadrants as a strong and honorable female. The term hard-ass has been used as well, but since she's siding with Creed and helping him stabilize the economy of our quadrant, I'll be gracious and go with strong and honorable.

Creed strides down the steps and meets the woman with his

hand outstretched. "Chancellor. Thank you for making time and coming right away."

The woman, an aged tree nymph with glasses and moss green hair is as elegant and sharp in her twilight years as anyone could hope for. I don't think Creed could have chosen a shrewder ally to oversee this project.

When the introductions are over, the six of us head inside and find Dune and a pretty brunette coming to greet us.

Huh, so this must be Mint Girl.

I study her and as much as I try not to let my claws come out, I don't see the appeal. She's got a stuffy librarian vibe to her, and Dune is much more a wild side kind of guy. Whatever. No accounting for past indiscretions, I suppose.

"Hello again, Chancellor," the brunette says, bowing her chin. "King Creed, Princess Honor, it's a pleasure to meet you. If you would follow me, I have everything set up in the meeting room."

Of course, she does.

Shadow

Doc, Demarco, and I spend the day discussing how the minds of oracles work, the physiology, the psychic energy, and the conscious thought. We take a lot of baseline tests so Doc can track my condition going forward. And by the end of it all, I've had enough.

"I don't want to seem ungrateful, gentlemen, but I'm tired of being under the microscope. Can we be done for now?"

Demarco nods and rises to his feet. "It's a nice day, why don't we go tour the grounds and get some fresh air. I bet your little wolf would welcome an outing and a change of scenery will be good for all of us."

I get up from the sofa, stiff from sitting too long in one position. "I'd like that, thank you."

Demarco nods. "Of course. I'm here to help you, Shadow, not force you into anything you don't want to do."

While I use the facilities, Doc visits the kitchen, and by the time the three of us are regrouping at the front door, Moonshade is bouncing with excitement and Doc is handing out bottles of ale. "I figured you could probably use a little alcoholic refreshment."

I accept the gift and take a long swallow. As the deep-bodied flavor cools its way down my throat and into my stomach, I take a moment to relax and regroup. "You figured right. Thank you."

The three of us walk for a while, enjoying the breeze in our faces and the utter joy Moonshade gets from her natural surroundings.

"So, this is Lukas's home. I admit it's not the kind of place I thought he would finally plant roots."

I glance at the draconian elder and wonder how he and Lukas know one another. "What makes you say that? If not here, then where did you see him finding his place?"

"In the decade I've known him, Lukas thrived in the city at Hawk Barron's side. He always seemed so at home in the jungle of concrete, steel, and glass."

"Home is where the heart is," Doc says, raising his beer. "Before Keyla, I was an ex-marine turned small-town doctor. I'm sure no one from my past would picture me as the mate of the royal couple living in the castle of a quadrant king."

Demarco nods. "Destiny weaves new opportunity into the fabric of our lives."

I think about that metaphor. "I could've used a little less weaving or maybe just the ability to pull the threads that made me blind and an oracle."

"I hear you." Demarco sighs, his attention drifting off into the distance.

Our footfalls mark the passage of time and place as the three of us wander the great outdoors.

The grounds of Amberloq Hall aren't as extensive as Thornebane Castle but they are private and are beginning to feel like home. There is an extensive section of forest that joins our property to the castle grounds. It almost completely hides the stone, four-story building we live in, but I'm told from a distance, the copper roof glimmers above the treetops.

Moonshade bounds past us in a wild run and I'm glad I have a hold on Doc's elbow, or my footing would definitely be affected by the onslaught of her vision. I'm not getting nauseous anymore, but I find her moving while I'm walking still affects my balance at times.

"That building over there is the training pavilion," Doc says. "And that structure by the pond is the meditation temple."

I wish I could see what he's pointing out. As the person who lives in this compound, I would like to be the one giving our guest the tour.

I suppose a blind tour guide isn't much good.

"Not to ruin the moment or anything," Doc says, "but have you two discussed the premonition? We're all still wound up about what it means to Creed as well as baby Ashborn. I don't mean to push, but there's a reason why Shadow's first oracle moment picked that as the message to be delivered. We need to figure out what it is."

The premonition he's asking about is not a premonition. It was the first prophecy I made after my transition to an oracle.

"Shadow mentioned the prophecy," Demarco says, "but we haven't started taking it apart. His physical well-being was my first concern."

"Oh, ours too," Doc says. "Please, don't get me wrong. We're all one hundred percent committed to Shadow's well-being as our priority. After that, we'd love to understand what's coming at us."

"You don't need to apologize," I say, squeezing Doc's elbow. "I understand the importance of facing what's coming at us. I want the missive to help the family. I simply don't know how to interpret it yet."

"All right, then let's hear it," Demarco says.

I hold up my beer and toast the group. *"The child of fire, the moon of light, A sea of blood to stain the night, The foe of freedom, the king is down, A war of outcasts to hold the crown."*

"And how much of that have you figured out?" Demarco asks.

"We figure it's a progression of unrelated events. We all agreed the child of fire refers to the birth of the phoenix baby last week."

"And since Ashborn came on the full moon, we figure that whole first line is complete," Doc says.

"That brings us to, A sea of blood to stain the night," I say.

"Wouldn't it be lovely if prophecies didn't always come out so dark and dire?" Demarco says. "Maybe something like, The storm has passed, the day is won, The girl of your dreams will soon come."

I chuckle. "That would be better. Next time, I'll try to prophesy something a little more upbeat."

"Yeah, you do that," Doc says. "Maybe there could be something in there about a beach holiday and lying around in the tropical surf."

"I'll do my best."

"So, on the list of what's to come," Demarco says, bringing us back on point, "we've got a night of bloodshed, the fall of the king, and then the army of outcasts turn the tides so Creed can hold the crown."

"That's the gist of it, yes."

"All right then. I don't think it's that dire."

Doc chuffs. "No? How do you figure?"

"It's basically saying there is a troubled time on the horizon, but everything works out. Bloodshed, the king falls, and then his outcasts hold the line and he regains the crown. All you have to do is wait this one out. You already know how it will turn out."

"Or maybe it's a self-fulfilling prophecy and there are things we're supposed to be doing to ensure the end result we're hoping for," Doc says.

"Maybe, but that's easy too. Who is your outcast army? Connect with them and get them rallied and ready to defend the crown."

"It would have to be the Amberloq survivors, wouldn't it?" Doc says. "We need to pull them back onside and solidify the army of Dornte."

"Possibly," Demarco says. "That's a great place to start, but prophecies are a tricky thing. They never flat-out tell you what you need to do. There's always some kind of deeper treasure you need to mine for."

He's not wrong. "One of the things my father hated most about my mother's people is that they could never just speak plainly."

"Mean what you say and say what you mean," Doc says.

"With oracles, things are never that simple."

CHAPTER SIX

Lukas

  or the next few days, the five of us keep to much the same schedule. Shadow and Demarco work on his oracle difficulties with the occasional help from Honor and Creed, Dune and Tundra assist Rhylan in the establishment of the Central Mint as the global economy site, and I try to keep my head in the game but mostly fail.

I'm so worried about Shadow it breaks my heart.

Not that anyone on the outside looking in would be able to tell. Well, other than my mates.

Honor senses my turmoil with her gifts and Tundra and Dune know me well enough to recognize my struggles. Still, I don't think Shadow has any idea how scared I am for him.

Having been through this once before, I know how bad it can get.

"I think I'll hang back with Shadow today," I say, over breakfast. The words come out casually as I pour myself a refill of tea. "You three don't need me at Valorous Hall and someone should probably stay here to receive everyone when they arrive. I'm thinking we'll chillax and lay out the welcome mat."

Shadow frowns. "Everything here is ready to receive. I planned to go with you."

Honor meets my gaze and shakes her head almost imperceptibly. "Well, if Shadow's going, you'd be here all by your lonesome. If you want some quiet time in solitude, that's fine."

My brow pinches and I run my fingers across my forehead. "You're going, Shadow? Are you sure that's a good idea?"

I regret the thick disapproval in my voice, but it's *not* a good idea. Demarco already warned me about not wrapping our poor elf in cotton and packing bubbles but I can't help it.

I run my thumb down the condensation building on the outside of my glass. "I assumed you'd stay home and thought I could keep you company."

Shadow draws a deep breath and I know he'll smell my worry and frustration, but there's nothing I can do about that. "That is both sweet and thoughtful. The truth is, I've been cooped up in here for the better part of the week and--"

"Because you collapsed," I say, my emotions getting the better of me. "If Demarco hadn't shown up and scooped you off the floor, who knows what might have happened."

"I know exactly what would've happened. I would've woken up, realized I'd passed out on the floor, and likely not mentioned it to you."

"Don't even joke about that."

"I'm not joking."

"Why wouldn't you tell us what happened?"

"To avoid a situation just like this one."

I take a beat and shut my mouth long enough for my logical mind to catch up. "I'm sorry. Please don't mistake what I said for anything other than concern. You need to tell us when things happen. We have to know."

"Why? Episodes of unconsciousness are common with

oracle transitioning. It's just my body succumbing to the overload at that moment. I've lived with this in the back of my mind my entire life. I know more about it than anyone else here. Don't forget, this is happening to *me*."

I squeeze his hand, my eyes stinging with the rising probability of tears. "I'm painfully aware of that."

"Then understand I need to remain a vital person. Passing out doesn't mean I have to spend the rest of my days locked away."

"You're not locked away. Is that how you feel?" I search his face, panic and regret overwhelming me.

Honor reaches over and rests her hand on my thigh. "Deep breath, magic man. Shadow's doing really well, and I'll be there if anything happens. This is a long-term situation and if Shadow wants to resume his connections with the outside world, he's more than welcome to join us."

I curse and take in the looks around the table. "It's not that I don't want you there. It's just—"

"It'll be fine," Tundra says, his voice soft and calm. "Shadow's right. His transition isn't who he is, it's something that happened to him. He could go for weeks or months without having an episode and it's not fair to try to contain his life."

"And don't forget," Dune says, "he's an incredible counselor, and the one hundred and seven Elbirfae men, women, and children who were held prisoner in that compound could benefit from someone with his qualifications."

The sadness I see reflected in the eyes of my mates tells me I've lost. "Of course, you're right. You're all right. I'm just being overprotective, I guess."

"And I love you for it," Shadow says, squeezing my hand, "but I need to do this. Bringing the survivors back into the fold is important for the prophecy, the rebuilding of the Amberloq, and the transitioning of the Elbirfae. It's also important for me. I can do this. I *need* to do this."

I let out a long-suffering breath. "Okay then. Let's finish eating and get going. The Elbirfae outcasts await."

~

Honor

My poor magic man. Lukas is so twisted up with his concerns for Shadow he can hardly be out of the room without glancing at the door every ten minutes.

I understand the impulse—I do—but having been the one who woke up from being tortured and tormented, I know what it's like to have people hovering and walking on eggshells around me.

I won't do that to Shadow.

Tundra's right. Shadow might not have another episode for weeks or months, so why borrow trouble and expect the worst. Besides, we have Demarco now and he seems to know a great deal about late-onset oracle genes firing to life.

I make a mental note to ask Lukas more about that. How did Demarco become our expert?

"Princess Honor. It's wonderful to see you." Lark, the warrior representative for the Forested Jungle Biome, is a fierce brunette with ebony wings and stunning emerald eyes.

She jogs down the front steps of my aunt's warrior hall and greets Lukas, Shadow, and me as we get out of the SUV. Dune and Tundra land beside us and she says hello to them as well.

"It's good to see you," I say. "I'm sorry we haven't been here in the last few days. A lot has happened."

"We saw the king's announcement. I bet that fired up all kinds of fireworks for you."

"It did. Still, I don't want you or the Elbirfae here to think we've forgotten about you. How are things?"

She waves away my concerns with the flick of her hand.

"Don't worry about that. It's easier not having strangers around while the children adjust to the idea of being safe."

I sigh. "I know that feeling too well. I'm sorry this happened to you."

"There's no use lamenting. It did happen and now we're here."

True. "About that. Now that the dust has settled, we'd like to invite you all to move into Amberloq Hall with us."

Her expression darkens. "You want to move us? Why? Amberloq Hall is for the royal warriors of the crown, not seniors, children, and those too injured or broken to fight."

"Usually, yes, but until we have a fighting force, we have plenty of room and thought being closer to the city would—"

Lark holds up her hand. "As much as I appreciate the sentiment, Princess, we're dealing with enough post-traumatic stress as it is. Moving everyone to another location with more people and the possibility of more castle raids would be the opposite of helpful."

"I assure you, Ruic Breard doesn't have the men or the means to attack the castle again. Also, if you lived with us, Shadow could spend time with those who need him. He's a counselor trained to help people navigate PTSD."

Lark shrugs and her wings flex behind her. "Why move a hundred people to access one man? Doesn't it make more sense to have him come here? Then, once you start repopulating the Amberloq numbers, you won't need to move us again."

"We considered that and were hoping the survivors might want to take advantage of everything the castle location has to offer."

"Very few Elbirfae thrive in the city centers. Historically, we live in remote locations in small pockets of community. The city doesn't hold as much appeal to them as you might expect."

I consider mentioning the prophecy and how the outcasts are meant to help save my brother's throne but considering I just told her the Elbirfae wouldn't have to worry about Ruic Breard causing trouble at the castle, that seems a little hypocritical.

"Fine. If you honestly don't think it would be a welcome move, of course, we won't do it."

Lark seems to relax a little. "Thank you, Princess. I know it makes things more difficult to have us out here, but I have to advocate for what I think is best for my people."

I raise a hand to stop her. "I understand you mean that in the most protective way, but they are *my* people as well. *I* am the Guardian of the Crown. My mates found you and we freed you. Please don't draw a line of division in the sand."

The two of us meet eye-to-eye and I see not only the aggression in her gaze but also the defiance of authority. "I understand that someone who has been through what you went through might not appreciate being challenged but if you expect to represent the forested jungle, you need to check that challenge of yours and realize I *am* in charge."

My words seem to sink in because she drops her gaze. "No, of course. I think I've been fighting for them for so long it's hard for me not to anticipate a fight at every turn. My apologies."

I gauge the sincerity of her words and am satisfied she's genuine. "Apology accepted. Now, since we're already here, Dune and Tundra want to ensure you have everything you need, Shadow would like to make himself available to anyone who needs counsel, and Lukas and I need time in my aunt's library."

She makes a face. "The library is one of the worst rooms in the entire building. Everything is rubble and ruin. I'm not sure what you're hoping to find in there, but I'm afraid you might be disappointed."

"Understood. There are some Guardian things I need to pick up if they are still intact."

"Miracles do happen."

"Yes, they do." I meet the gaze of my mates and we head inside.

It's maddening to me that the only time I've been in my aunt's home—the place where she managed and lived among the Amberloq warriors—is after she died.

Even if she and my father didn't get along, I was her successor. She should've gotten over herself and made things right for a smooth transition of power.

She didn't.

But as Lark said outside. There's no use lamenting. It happened and this is where we are.

"It's the same floorplan as Amberloq Hall," Lukas says, glancing around. "That's not weird at all."

I'm as taken back as he is.

Dune and Tundra have been here quite regularly, and I was here when we first dropped everyone off, but I didn't come inside.

Maybe it was me not wanting Valorous to disappoint me again, or maybe I've simply neglected the Elbirfae survivors.

Whatever the reason, it's weird now.

"The good news is we know exactly where to find the library."

Lukas nods and falls into step with me and Moonshade. "Come on, girl. You know where we're going, don't you?"

Shadow chuckles behind me. "Honestly, she thinks you're on your way to the kitchen and she's hoping for a treat."

I laugh. "Sorry, little wolf. Not yet. When we get home, I'll get you something. I promise."

Lukas, Shadow, Moonshade, and I make our way into my aunt's library, and I stop in the middle of the room. "Wow, Lark wasn't kidding. This place is trashed beyond all recognition."

"There are no shelves left and no little black mirrors where a DNA scanner should be. How are you going to get into her vault?"

"I have no idea."

I glance around the area where the DNA mirror is located in our library and groan. "Why did the one difference in the two spaces have to be the key that unlocks the Guardian Chronicles?"

Lukas chuckles. "Murphy's Law."

Shadow picks up Moonshade and the three of us wander around, searching for a hidden entrance to a Guardian Library or a switch to trip or something that leads us to her hidden stash of discs.

"Nothing," I say after twenty minutes of searching. "If there was something, it's not here now."

"Shit. I'm sorry, babe." Lukas tromps over the debris-cluttered floor to come hug me. "I know how much it means to you to have your aunt's wisdom to guide you on this journey."

It does. "Maybe it's stupid considering all the discs I got from all the other wonderful women, but yeah, I had big hopes for what Valorous might have to say."

"What are you looking for?" a teenage blond girl with snowy white wings asks.

I recognize the girl from the compound where we found and rescued everyone in the Badlands. "Skye, isn't it?"

The girl nods.

I gesture to her and then my mates. "Lukas and Shadow, this is Skye. Tundra described her as a little sister of sorts from his village in the snowy peaks."

"It's a pleasure to meet you, Skye," Shadow says.

"Any friend of Tundra's is a friend of ours," Lukas says. "We're glad you survived your ordeal."

"Thank you. Listen, I…uh, overheard you talking with Lark earlier when you first got here. Even if most of us want to stay here, she doesn't actually speak for all of us. Some of the guys want to become Amberloq and Tundra is my family. I'd like to go too."

I meet the girl's gaze and then check in with Lukas and Shadow. "Thanks for letting me know. We'll talk to Lark again and I'll have Tundra come talk to you once we figure out what's best."

Her expression lights up.

"Don't say anything yet, okay," I add. "We don't want to ruffle any feathers or cause any trouble for the others. Just leave it with us and we'll talk more about it before we go. Does that sound fair?"

Skye nods. "Fair. I won't say a word, Princess."

CHAPTER SEVEN

Tundra

*D*une and I take two of the young males to the closest village to get supplies. One boy, River, is from the forest biome and has the brilliant blue feathers of a hyacinth macaw and the other, Danner, has the sandy brown falcon wings of the desert plains.

"So, you're holding tryouts to be Amberloq, right?" Danner asks, flying on my right. "We saw a media announcement about it. We missed a lot of things while we were prisoners, but we didn't miss our chance, right?"

"No. You haven't missed that. We only posted the announcement a couple of weeks ago. With the rebels trying to overtake King Creed's rule, we haven't moved forward with getting the tournament ready."

"Yet," Dune says. "It's going to be epic though. Princess Honor put Tundra and me in charge. Since we're the only two living Amberloq left, we're the only ones who know the tests and trials from before."

"What about the elders," River asks, looking confused. "Flint and Talon told us lots of stories while we were captured. They might be old now, but they were Amberloq when they were young."

I fight not to laugh at the look of indignation on Dune's face. Apparently, he forgot about those who came before and truly believed we were the only two. "We will, of course, take their council and include them in the planning. We always benefit from the knowledge and experience of our elders."

"Yeah, of course," Dune says. "We've been alone in this so long, I guess I didn't think about the elders from the compound."

"How did you two survive, anyway?" Danner asks.

"We were on an away assignment," Dune says.

River brightens. "The universe spared you. Perhaps you two were meant to bring the Amberloq back from the brink."

"Another rise from the ashes," Danner says. "Did you guys hear that the Phoenix rose? She opened the Portal Gate to the Human Realm too."

"I can't believe we missed that," River says.

"Only by a few months," I say, shifting my wings to descend toward the local store. "The gate isn't even at full capacity for travel yet. With the rebels still causing trouble, we're being quite strict about who comes and goes."

"We? As in, you guys are part of the action?"

The excitement exuding from them is heartwarming. I remember when I was a youth and had that same untamed enthusiasm.

We land at the grocery and supply store and the four of us head inside. Dune and I stop as the door closes behind us, and I know it hits him too.

"It's the smell, isn't it?"

Dune nods.

"What's the smell?" Danner asks. "Do you smell danger? Is it blood? What do you smell?"

Dune's brow arches and he chuckles. "Dial it down a notch, sapling. We were just reminiscing. Tundra and I were sent here a hundred times for supplies. The smell of the store's interior just brought back a rush of memories. That's all."

The boys look crestfallen.

I hand them each a packing box from inside the door. "Canned vegetables, beans, and soups on the bottom row and then a row of pasta, and top it with eggs and bread. We'll get the meat, produce, and treats."

When the boys shuffle off, I meet Dune's gaze and chuckle. "Were we ever that excited about the prospect of battle?"

Dune laughs. "I don't know about you, but I was."

I think about that. "Yeah, I was too."

"As I live and breathe," an elderly woman says behind me. "I gave you two up fer dead years back."

We turn to find the matriarch of this little village eyeing us up and down. "Hello, Granny Gray. It's good to see you."

She waves her hands and reels us in for a hug. The woman stands less than five feet, so we have to double over, but we do our best. "It's good to be seen. Imagine, the two of you lived through the horrors and even kept from killin' one another."

Dune laughs. "I know. That seems even less likely."

"Gall, the way the two of you used to go at it."

Dune waggles his brows at me, and his double entendre is wholly inappropriate. As well as untrue. The two of us never started 'going at it' until being locked up together for ages.

"Oh, he pretended he was going to rip me to shreds, but even back then he loved me. Didn't you?"

I give him a droll stare. "No. Back then I would absolutely have slit your throat if it wasn't against every law I lived by."

Dune chuckles. "It's a fine line between love and hate."

"Well, that explains so much."

Granny Gray follows the conversation from Dune to me and

back again, her head pivoting. "What's this? Are you boys a thing now?"

I nod. "We are now mated to each other and Princess Honor as her Biome Generals. A lot has changed in two years."

Dune chuckles. "Don't let him fool you, GG. All that blustering and fury was him compensating for loving me even then."

I roll my eyes. "It absolutely was not. You are less of an acquired taste and more a parasite that I couldn't shake and eventually gave up trying."

"Harsh. That hurts my feelings, frosty."

I don't think it actually does, but with Dune, he hides his true feelings so well, I can't be sure. Deciding to make up for my last comment I lean sideways and kiss his cheek. "You know I love you."

His smile is too sweet and goofy for words. "Yeah, you do."

The boys are finished in the canned food aisle and heading for the pasta. "It's been lovely catching up with you, Granny Gray. If you'll excuse us, we have to get shopping and get back."

Granny gestures for us to carry on. "Shop away, my boys. It's wonderful to have so many mouths to feed again."

Dune

We get the boys and the groceries back to the Elbirfae and Honor comes out to greet us on the lawn. "Hello, mates. How goes your checklist of things to do?"

I laugh. "We got groceries, met up with a local elder for a few chuckles at Tundra's expense, and got our ears chatted off by two of the most enthusiastic Amberloq hopefuls ever."

"Speaking of hopeful youths, I need to talk to you, Tundra."

"Should I be concerned?"

"Tundra, dude," I say, shaking my head. "Just because

someone wants to speak with you doesn't mean you need to hit the panic button. Chillax."

He looks at me like I've grown a few extra heads and gone hydra. "You need to stop hanging out with Brant."

"Hells no. Brant's the best. I love that big teddy bear."

Honor waves to us and blinks. "Hello, remember me? I'm the one trying to have a conversation with you?"

Tundra straightens. "Apologies, Princess. What were you saying about hopeful youths?"

"First of all, Lark shut down our idea of moving everyone to Amberloq Hall. She said they're settled here and not interested in getting closer to the bustle of the city and the people there."

"Does she speak for all of them?" Dune asks.

"Apparently not. We've had a request from Skye to come live with us. She considers you her closest family and wants to move in."

"Just until we have Amberloq living there?" Tundra asks. "And then what happens to her?"

"I don't think that's what she's hoping for. I think she's looking to become part of your—and by extension our—family."

"But no one other than the warriors live in Amberloq Hall."

"In Valorous's day, that was true. In my reign, we're already going to have Lukas, Shadow, and Moonshade. If Skye has a place in your life, we can certainly accommodate her."

"But what happens when there are three-hundred men in that house? She's just a young girl. That hardly seems appropriate."

Honor smiles. "You're worried about the girl's honor and reputation?"

"Shouldn't I be? As you said, I'm the closest thing she has to family."

"Well, having been raised in a castle with several hundred guards and citizens, I can say that a parent can only ever do so much to ward off suitors. In the end, Skye will make up her own mind about who she wants to spend time with."

Tundra scowls. "I don't like that one bit."

I pat his shoulder and squeeze. "I've got your back, T. We can put the fear of death into any males prowling after her. Trust me, I know all the signs and all the lines."

Honor shakes her head. "You two are incorrigible. My question is whether or not you wish to take on the role of her guardian, not if you think you can police her life. Besides, what if she wants to become an Amberloq Warrior herself?"

"*What!?* That's just crazy talk." My mind catches up with my outburst a little too late. I see the look on Honor's face shift and the hackles on the back of my neck start to rise. "I meant...of course, female Amberloq warriors. Why not, right?"

"Exactly right, Dune. Good save."

I run my fingers through my hair and shake out my wings. "Thanks. I may be thick and mouthy, but I'm learning."

Honor smiles at me and I know I barely escaped that one.

"I think Calli, Keyla, Lark, and I have proven that women can hold their own in battle."

"Without a doubt, Princess," Tundra says.

"And since we already agreed we are changing the requirements to join the Amberloq force, allowing women to apply makes perfect sense."

Tundra shakes out his wings and tries to gather himself. "In theory, I agree. In reality, I don't like the idea of Skye setting her sights on being a warrior. She has always been a sweet and gentle soul."

Honor takes his hand and squeezes. "The young woman she is today might not be the same as the girl you left behind in your village two years ago. My point was to probe whether or not you are opting for the task of taking her under your wing."

Tundra nods. "If she wants to be with me, I could and would never turn her away. She is my—"

"Yes! Thank you!" Skye comes bounding over a wide spruce tree and lands in the center of our conversation circle. The moment her feet touch the ground, she throws herself at Tundra and wraps herself around him. "You won't regret it. I swear I'll be good, and you won't have to kill boys, and I have no plans on being a warrior."

Tundra frowns. "Is there any part of our private conversation you didn't listen to?"

She eases back and blinks up at him. "Sorry. I was excited. *Annnd* from now on, I won't eavesdrop."

He chuckles and shakes his head. "What have I agreed to?"

~

Honor

It's well past midday when I track down Lark in the common room and signal for her to join me in the entrance hall for a private chat. We had a bit of a bumpy morning and I want to make sure we're on the same page moving forward.

"Are you heading out?" she says, maybe a little too eagerly not to be offended.

"Very soon, but first, I want to speak to everyone as a group."

Her gaze narrows. "Of course. You want to extend your support and pep talk the troops. I get it."

"Yes, that, and I'm going to invite anyone who wishes to come to Amberloq Hall to join us."

She takes a step back and her gaze darkens. "We discussed this. Upheaval isn't what's best for them."

I gesture to where Shadow is leaning with his shoulder against the wall in the entranceway. "He's a trained professional and has spoken to close to forty people today and doesn't share your assessment."

Lark scoffs. "And what? You think a ten-minute conversation gives him more insight into this group than me?"

"I do. We've had several members of this community come to us, asking us what's next for them. Several more have flat out asked to come to Amberloq Hall to live and apply to be warriors for the crown."

"You mean the kids. They don't know what's best for them. Sure, they're impassioned to fight after the past two years and excited to be free to make choices, but they don't understand what those choices mean."

"And that's what the trials and training of the Amberloq are about."

She shakes her head. "I realize you don't see what I see, but this group has been a tight unit through two years of hell. You can't just remove members without leaving holes in the lives of the others. I can't allow that."

My wings release behind me and I straighten to my full height. "You don't *allow* me to do anything. I am the fucking Guardian of the Crown and the innocents within the quadrant of Dornte are *my* responsibility. In a horrible situation, you asserted yourself as their protector and leader. Well done. I applaud you for your accomplishment."

"I didn't do it for your applause."

"No. You did what you needed to do to protect them, but that time has passed. You are imposing your wishes and your fears on them by trying to keep them prisoner here. I can't allow that."

Her emerald eyes flare as I accuse her of holding them prisoner.

"You might not see it that way, but to keep even one person from moving forward because you refuse to let them move on is just another kind of imprisonment. Now, set your ego aside, shut your mouth, and I will have my say. And if you don't like it, keep in mind that this is *my* property and *my* roof over your head and *my* credits buying your groceries. Don't try to bully me, female. You weren't the only one imprisoned and tortured for the last two years. I understand more than you think I do."

By the time I finish, my voice is echoing off the hard surfaces in the entrance foyer and the house has gone quiet.

Fucking hell. I stare Lark down and luckily for her, she keeps her mouth shut. "Shadow, you're with me."

I hold my arm out to him. He has Moonshade in his arms and they walk with me back to the Great Room. "I'm sorry for the drama everyone. You have two very strong-willed females fighting for your well-being and Lark and I don't agree on the next steps."

I offer her what I hope is an understanding smile, but she's not having any of it.

Maybe she just needs time to simmer down.

"As you very likely heard. I want to invite any of you who wish to move to Amberloq Hall to join us on the castle grounds. Whether you hope to become an Amberloq warrior, have an interest in the city, or want to stay for a time and explore a world denied to you for far too long, you are welcome."

"And if we don't want to go?" A snowy peaks elder asks. "What does that look like?"

"Nothing at all. If you are happy where you are, then you stay here as long as you wish. Whether that is for the rest of your time in this world or until you return to your biomes, it doesn't matter. There is no rush for you to do anything."

"Is it true what you said?" a woman asks from the end of one of the couches. "Were you imprisoned and tortured like us?"

I draw a deep breath and steady myself. As much as I hate thinking about that time, with each day that passes, it fades further into my past.

"I can't say if our experiences were the same. I was captured during the raid on the castle and forced to watch as my parents were slaughtered. I was a body to abuse by the guards. I was spelled by the Blood Witch, locked in my own mind, and buried in a bunker sealed inside a lead vault. I don't discount anything done to any of you. I simply want to offer a way to move forward for those who are ready."

"And we truly don't have to leave?" a thirty-something male with one leg asks.

"You truly don't. Valorous Hall is yours to use for as long as you wish. We will continue to check-in. I will continue to ensure you have what you need. And in time, when you figure out what you want from this life, Creed and I will help you rebuild."

"Thank you, Princess," Lark says, from the doorway. Back straight and chin up, she's an imposing sight. "Your offer is generous. I apologize for forgetting my place. My emotions clouded my judgment."

I nod. "During my first weeks after being rescued, I was angry too. No matter how often the people around me assured me I was safe, I didn't believe it—I couldn't. I wasn't easy to be around. It takes time."

With that said, I draw a deep breath and gesture to the door. "My mates and I will wait out by our vehicle. Talk among yourselves and feel no pressure. If today is not your day for moving on, the offer remains open going forward. For those of you who asked about joining us, get your things and meet us outside. We will be happy to have you."

And with that, I hook my arm with Shadow's, and Lukas, Dune, and Tundra fall in behind me as we march out to the entrance and out to our SUV.

CHAPTER EIGHT

Lukas

*T*oday marks a new chapter in the lives of my mates. In the air above the SUV fly twenty young men and women who chose to come learn about being Amberloq Warriors. Skye is there too, delighted to reunite with Tundra. In the back seat sit Terran and Ambrose, retired Amberloq elders dedicated to rebuilding the force they love. And in the middle seat next to Shadow sits Rivka, a tribal cook from the desert plains who intends on being the den mother to the group.

I glance back at the sun-kissed female with warm, brown eyes. She insists it's her duty to join us and cook for Dune.

We tried to explain to Dune that no one should feel beholden to cook for him, even if he *is* her Biome representative. He disregarded our frustrations saying we don't understand the ways of the nomadic desert communities.

According to him, to refuse her offer, would be a life-destroying blow stealing away her purpose as a useful member of society.

We didn't know how to argue with that.

So, in the end, we accepted her offer and are pleased she'll be with us to help care for the kids.

"Are you sure you're okay?" I whisper to Honor, asking for the second time.

The ride home from Valorous Hall has been a quiet one. Our princess regrets losing her temper with Lark and causing a scene. I told her she wasn't wrong to do so, but she regrets it just the same.

In my opinion, Lark needed to be reminded we are not the enemy and she's not in charge.

I reach across to her seat and squeeze her hand. "It all worked out in the end."

Moonshade lets off a series of quiet yips and I lift my gaze to the rear-view mirror. The little wolf is curled up in Shadow's lap sound asleep. Shadow brushes a hand over her side and then reclines his seat a little to join her in slumber.

He looks pale and tired.

Guilt spears me.

Say what you want about multiple partner relationships, the truth is, there are times we don't get much sleeping done in our bed.

Working with Demarco and practicing the mental exercises he's teaching Shadow is exhausting. I know they are. We would totally understand if Shadow needed to opt-out of a night of play or wanted to start napping in the afternoon.

He won't because he knows we'd worry.

But taking a nap in the truck is perfectly normal.

I ease off the gas a little and decide not to be in a rush to get back to the castle. He may not want to look weak and sick in front of us, but the truth is, his body is going through something and any extra rest I can give him is a good thing.

Honor notices me studying the rear-view mirror and glances back. "He needs more rest," she whispers.

"I was thinking the same thing."

"How is it that Demarco is an expert on late-onset oracle genes?"

I meet her gaze and shrug. "It's not my story to tell, but the gist of it is that his daughter was in the same situation once and he tried to help her."

"Once? It ended?"

I sigh and a little more life drains out of me. "Tragically, I'm afraid."

Honor's expression softens as that sinks in. "This must be so difficult for him."

"That's why I wasn't sure he would help us. I certainly didn't expect him to come to the Fae Realm and move in with us."

"But I'm thankful he did."

"Me too."

We drive for another long while before Honor breaks the silence again. "How did you get involved?"

I was wondering how long it would take for her to get there. "Alyssa, his daughter, and I had a casual fondness for one another. When I found out she was suffering, I tried to help. Demarco and I did everything we could to get help from the Ordained Oracles, but they wouldn't even hear us out."

"Did they know the girl was suffering?"

"They knew. Oracles are an intractable bunch. They are so set in their practices of how to raise a child with their powers they refuse to consider anyone who falls out of that scope."

"That's awful."

"It's arrogant and negligent, but what was awful was the way Alyssa suffered as her mind fractured bit by bit."

I grip the steering wheel tighter and glance back at Shadow. The soft snore of his sleep makes me smile. "This time will be different. Demarco never stopped learning about how the oracle genes overwrite the mind. His obsession has served to help others since."

Honor reaches over and squeezes my arm. "Creed and I will

learn what we need to do to keep his mind from fracturing, I swear."

"I believe that. And I also think Shadow's got an advantage because he's an elf and a counselor."

"Yeah? What does that have to do with it?"

"Meditation and mindfulness are part of his daily life. He already orders his thoughts more than others do. He is skilled at understanding his impulses and content to spend quiet time reflecting."

Honor nods. "I'm sure once he—"

Shadow pikes forward with a hiss and Moonshade yips and starts growling.

I look into the rear-view mirror and my heart cleaves in two. "Fuck."

The truck swerves to the shoulder, and I slam the gear shift into park and bail out my door. I've got the passenger door open and am grabbing his flailing arms as his eyes flip open and those freaky opal pupils practically start glowing.

"It's okay, Shadow. I've got you."

"Let me get to him," Honor says, bodychecking me out of the way as she leans into the truck. She clasps both hands against his temples and closes her eyes. "It's okay, sweetie. We're here."

"What's happening?" Dune says, landing beside me. "Oh no. Not again."

"How bad is it?" Tundra lands with us and then the Elbirfae kids who want to claim a place as Amberloq Warriors touch down as well.

I rake my fingers through my hair and go sit on the back bumper of the truck before my rubbery legs give out. "I don't know. He jolted out of sleep and started convulsing."

"It's a vision," Honor says. "Connected like this, I can see it. Ruic and his men are going after the mint."

Fuckety-fuck.

I force myself back to my feet and pull myself together.

"Tundra and Dune, get to the mint now. I'll send you reinforcements."

"Princess?" Tundra asks, "are you with us?"

"No. I'll stay with Shadow until I'm sure his mind is secure. We'll check in once we get to the castle. Go."

They launch into the air, and I turn back to the truck's interior. Shadow has stopped seizing and I pray that means this is over or will be soon.

Flipping my wrist, I call up Rhylan on my tactical watch. When the call connects, I break in before he speaks. "Rhy, we have reason to believe Breard is mounting an attack on the Central Mint. I've sent Tundra and Dune, but Honor and I can't leave Shadow. I have a tactical team on site but not enough men if he's mounting a takedown."

"On it. I'll take care of it."

The line drops and I turn to round up the kids… only there are no kids.

Did they follow Tundra and Dune into battle?

Fuckety-fuck.

Tundra

Dune and I are racing through the skies, pumping our wings hard to get to StoneHaven when I realize we're not alone. I glance back at the twenty young men and women flying at our heels. "You can't follow us," I shout. "We're going into battle."

"Yes, the two of you," River says. "Two of you against a goblin attack force. You may not like it, but you need us."

"We need soldiers, not civilians."

Skye pushes forward and gives me a dirty look. "We're not ordinary civilians, Tundra. We've trained every day for two years. Ambrose and Terran taught us strategy and defense. Lark,

Glenn, Clover, Fox, Bay, they all worked with us at every opportunity honing our fighting skills and making us stronger."

I hate the idea that Skye, the sweet young girl I knew from my village in the snowy peaks has spent the past two years fighting for survival.

"Still. We've never fought with you. It's dangerous to have the first time working as a team be during a battle."

"Don't be stupid." She rolls her eyes and peels off, falling back in the flight grouping.

"I don't speak teenager, but I think that means your conversation is over," Dune says, chuckling. "You have quite a way with her."

I peg him with a look and shake my head. "Like you could've done any better."

"I could have because I wouldn't have tried to forbid them to join us. They're right. We don't know what they're capable of and they're old enough and have been through enough to decide for themselves."

"No, they aren't, and no they haven't."

Dune laughs. "If you say so. In the desert nomad community, no one forced anyone to assume responsibility. When we felt ready to take more on, we were allowed the opportunity. No one ever told us we couldn't do anything."

I laugh. "I'm not surprised. That's probably one of the main reasons you think yourself able to do anything. You're *not*, by the way."

"You're one cranky guy, Iceman. You better start working on your bedside manner. You've inherited a teenager."

Now it's me who's peeling off to the side and rolling my eyes. Dropping toward the area of StoneHaven that recently became the center for a realm-wide economy, I am ready for the battle ahead.

And I'm not cranky.

Am I?

~

Dune

Watching Tundra flounder as an uptight father figure is going to be a hoot. Sure, he's a good guy underneath all that pent-up anal rigidness, but what teen in their right mind would choose him as their guardian when they had a tight-knit community already in place loving them?

Doesn't make sense to me.

Sadly, there's no time to dwell on that. We're approaching the Central Mint and there are six large trucks kicking up dust trails and barreling toward the building.

I tuck my wings back and drop toward the building as quickly as gravity and aerodynamics can take me. I catch up to Tundra and match the speed of his descent. "I know it's horrible that Shadow's suffering and all that, but these visions could come in handy. Don't you think?"

Tundra arches a brow at me. "All premonitions show something worth knowing. It would be silly for the fae universe to send us a message that you like pudding."

"It would...because I hate pudding."

"You're being intentionally obtuse."

"How about we focus on the moment at hand?" I ask, eyeing up the convoy of trucks almost within range. "We don't know how many fighters are down there or what kind of weapons they might have."

Wind whips at my face. If I weren't an Elbirfae, my eyes would be streaming from the force of the flow. But I am...so they're not.

"Okay, listen up, kids," I shout, loud enough so they hear me. "Goblins are greedy and cutthroat but lack the brainpower to impress the world with their intelligence. Fight strategically and if you get the chance to outsmart them, take it. Odds are they won't see it coming."

"What if it's not just the goblins?" Danner asks. "What if they've got those acid-spitting toad men?"

I blink. "I'm not familiar with the acid-spitting toad men. Care to elaborate?"

Danner judges the distance between us and the ground and gives me the short version. "If they're here. Their eyes glow gold and bug out before they spit. Don't let the spit hit you. It melts everything it touches."

"Charming."

Tundra lands first and touches down next to the FCO soldiers. Lukas stationed two squadrons here for the next few weeks until production gets up and running.

I land closer to the front walk and address the kids. "It's not your job to take on the oncoming force. The fact that you're here and filling out our numbers is good. Tundra and I will be first-line defense with the tactical teams already here. You guys are in charge of the entrances. Make sure no one gets inside, and no one inside gets hurt. Got it?"

River frowns at me. "We can do more than watch the doors."

"Excellent. I'm counting on it. Now, can you follow orders? Warrior Lesson Number 1: following the chain of command is a huge part of working with a warrior team. When you don't, people die."

That seems to settle him down a little. "Yes, sir."

"Perfect. This mint is more important than any one of us. Dornte needs this global currency to get out from under the goblins. Three of you on the side door, three more on the back, three more inside, and the rest of you on the main entrance. Got it?"

"Got it," Skye says, calling out names and locations.

"And keep your wings up and yourselves shielded. I mean it.

Honor will rip us all new orifices if you kids get banged up or killed on your first day with us."

"Take positions," one of the FCO officers shouts.

The trucks have arrived and the tires skid to a stop on the rocky ground. In the next moment, the doors fly open, and goblins hemorrhage out of the vehicles firing blasters.

I bring my wing up and wrap it around to shield my face. "Shields up. Take your positions. I'll toss weapons to you as we acquire them. Be ready kids. And good luck."

I was expecting the reality of the moment to catch up with them and the panic to set in. There's no sign that it's happening.

Maybe they were right, and their situation really did condition them for this better than we thought.

The first bolts of energy zing overhead and I get my wing up to block the incoming attack.

"Here we go."

CHAPTER NINE

Honor

I t seems like ages before Shadow regains consciousness and by then, my mind is on Tundra and Dune and whether or not the vision is coming true. I should be there with them...but Shadow needed me, and I should be with him too.

It's hell to need to be two places at once.

"Creed, what's happening?" I ask my brother as we're turning onto the castle property.

"The battle at the mint started a few minutes ago. Rhylan is a few minutes out. Lukas's teams are there with Tundra, Dune, and he said the kids? What kids? Does that make sense to you?"

"Yeah, the Elbirfae kids who were coming back with us to live at Amberloq Hall. When things went south, they followed Dune and Tundra before we realized they were gone."

"Tundra and Dune will watch out for them," Lukas says, flashing his headlights and honking at the security staff manning the gate.

Thankfully, they take the hint and get the traffic arm up

before we get there. The SUV zooms through the gate and Lukas doesn't stop until we get to the castle parking lot.

"Shadow, are you okay to take our guests back to Amberloq Hall?" I ask, torn between now needing to be in three places: the battle, the castle control room, and with Shadow.

"Of course, sweeting. Go be the Guardian of the Crown. Be safe. I love you."

I give him a quick kiss and point to the copper roof visible over the tops of the trees. "See that building in the distance? That's Amberloq Hall. Shadow will take you home. I'm sorry this is your welcome."

"It's fine, Princess," the tall desert nomad, Ambrose, says. "Your mate is right. Go be our guardian."

Lukas and I race toward the closest door of the castle and the guards open things up when they see us coming. "If we had someone with portalling abilities, we'd be on our way to Stone-Haven and not playing the part of overwatch."

"If you want to go, that's your call."

"Sure, I could fly there but the fight will likely be done before I arrive." We run through the castle, past the ID scanners, and down into the lower level to access the war room.

"Good, you're here," Creed says, tossing me and Lukas each a headset. "Rhylan is two minutes out. See if you can find Ruic Breard either at the battle site or anywhere else. I'm not convinced attacking the mint isn't a diversionary ploy."

Lukas jogs over to one of the consoles and starts plugging into one of the systems. "I'll take the battle and my guys can be my eyes on the ground. Honor, start up the facial and voice recognition software. Maybe we'll get lucky and the arrogant asshole will start bragging to someone that he's making a move."

The three of us spend the next few minutes getting locked in on the search for Ruic Breard.

He wouldn't be stupid enough to come out of hiding to attack the mint, would he?

As stupid as goblins are, Ruic doesn't fall into that category.

He's ruthless and driven.

I want him to be at the raid battle, but so far no one has spotted him, so Creed's likely right and he's up to something else.

"I'm so tired of Ruic Breard and his one-percent assholes," I say, mostly to myself.

"You and me both, sister," Creed says, bringing up a new view on the cameras at the Central Mint property. "Once again, Lukas, your enforcers are saving our Dornte Quadrant asses."

"Not for long. Look at these kids fight." He points to the screen of the monitor he's working on and eases back so we can see. "There's some serious skill here. If we work with them, they'll be battle-ready in a few months. All they need is some discipline and some tactical strategy."

I glance over at the battle in progress and smile. The Elbirfae young are guarding the entrances to the buildings and kicking the asses of any stray goblins that happen to get behind the primary force.

"It's incredible what the need to survive can do for people, isn't it? It really tests the steel of a person's convictions."

As we watch, Rhylan swoops in and spews a long line of flame, cutting off the goblins from their vehicles and any chance of escape. Whatever happens, there won't be any running away this time.

And there won't be any second chances.

I pull up the chipping information from the castle raid and am disappointed to see how many of the men at the mint were also involved in the raid here at the castle a few weeks ago.

"Stupid idiots. We gave them a second chance and they still chose to be part of Ruic's crew."

"How many of them were here for the castle raid?" Creed asks.

"Twenty-three."

"Well, it sucks to be them," Lukas says. "We made it very clear that we'd be able to track their involvement, so lock in their tracking information. They're done."

I sigh and start that process. What's upsetting is seeing their personal profiles. "Is coming at us really worth destroying their families?"

"There are no winners in war, babe," Lukas says. "Not your fault."

"No, it's not," Creed says. "It's Ruic's. So, let's find the fucker and take him down."

"I like the sound of that, but so far, it hasn't been that easy."

Creed shrugs. "Then we just keep hammering away at it until it's done. There's no way his supporters will keep backing him going forward. He lost his try for the castle. He lost his attack on us. And now he's lost his hold on Dornte's economy. He's got to be getting desperate."

Lukas nods and pegs us with a serious look. "There are few things more dangerous than a man who has nothing to lose. Don't count him down and out until he's in custody or dead."

"Preferably the latter," Creed says.

It might sound harsh, but I agree with him.

Dead is better.

Tundra

The battle is barely underway when Rhylan's mighty dragon form blocks out the sun and casts a monstrous shadow across the grounds of the Central Mint. I hear the gasp of one of the kids and shout over our shoulder. "The dragon is on our side. Focus on your tasks."

In truth, they're doing very well.

Dune tasked them to protect the building and let us run the

offense. I'm pleased with how well they've followed those instructions.

I'm also pleasantly surprised.

If the excitement of Danner and River was any indication of their enthusiasm, these kids are burning to regain the control they lost during their imprisonment. That's a hard thing to lock down when you're ordered to dial it back.

"Toad men!" one of the kids shouts and I check to see where they're indicating.

Wow, there are, indeed, eerily odd men dropping out of the back of one of the trucks.

And yes, they do have a squat stature and leathery, amphibious curves to their wide face and bodies. And at less than five feet tall and dressed in form-fitting leathers that do nothing for their shape, they do resemble large toads.

"Watch out for the acid spit!" one of the kids shouts. "It'll eat through your wings."

Dune flashes a look of horror. "Seriously? We can repel magic spells, and lasers, and rocket launcher missiles but toad spit will burn through our wings?"

"Since they have experience with the creatures and we don't, I suggest we take their council."

"Sure. That works." Dune rushes forward to one of the conveyance vehicles in the parking lot and grabs the handle. With a massive heave, he yanks the door and snaps it off the hinging mechanism. "Here, catch."

He tosses the awkward rectangle of glass and steel to me and moves on to the other door.

Another great heave and the two of us have matching, multi-layered metal shields with windows.

"Their spit is acid, but what about their blood?" I shout to the youths.

"No idea. No one in the compound ever got close enough to find out."

Well, that's not encouraging at all.

Dune and I advance as one and the FCO Enforcers open their defensive line to give us access to the incoming toad men.

"If we can force them over toward the open parking lot, Rhylan can get a clean shot at frying them," I say, pointing to the spot I mean.

"Then melt the butter because we're about to have all the frog's legs we can handle."

I chuff. "They look more like toads than frogs. Look how warty they are."

"Yeah, but fried toad's legs isn't a thing. It had to be frog's legs to make sense."

"How about you just slecking kill them?" River shouts from where he and the others are guarding the building entrance.

"Yeah, yeah," Dune says, shifting his focus to the incoming troop of toad men. "Warrior Lesson Number 2: battle can be grueling. Try to amuse yourself and your fellow warriors."

I scowl at him. "That is not a warrior lesson."

"It should be."

I shake my head. "Ignore him. Wise-cracking during battle is not a warrior lesson."

"Watch his eyes," a forest biome female shouts. "When they bulge and start to glow, and his throat goes weird like that, it means he's about to spit!"

The toad man closest to us lets off a moist hacking noise and parts his lips.

His mouth must be hinged to open wide because his lower jaw falls practically to his chest. At the same time the hacking noise starts, his throat constricts, and then bloats up.

Anticipating the spit coming for us, I rush forward, ducking behind my door shield as I charge.

There's a tinny *thunk* and then a long, slow sizzling hiss follows. I slow my attack as the steel of the car door dissolves beside my head. I glare at the hole that burns through both the inner and outer layers of the car door and eats everything in between.

And the stench...

Sweet mercies, it's unbelievable.

"Slecking hell, that's rank," Dune says, his face screwed up as if he's choking down chunks of sour milk. "That's really bad."

The two of us make it to the first toad men and I swing my shield as a weapon. It's tricky to wield now because toad spit is still dripping and flinging and burning through things.

A few wayward drops catch my arm and land on my pants and yeah, it hurts like hell as it singes my skin beneath.

"Why didn't you kids warn us about the stink?" Dune asks.

"Because the smell won't kill you, but the acid will," one of them shouts.

Makes sense.

Drops of melted metal splat onto the pavement of the parking lot and melt the ground to a black goo. "Be careful. Even after it's expelled it's still eating through everything."

Dune switches his grip on the door to swing it like a giant steel blade. He gets a lucky swing and slices the heads off the first two men and then lifts it back to use as a shield as the next in line start to bulge and bloat.

I study the cutting edge of Dune's door shield. "The blood doesn't seem to have the same corrosive effect as the acid spit does."

"That's one good thing."

The rolling heads give the other toad men a scare and they stop advancing.

The two of us, continue swinging, forcing them back to the empty spot in the parking lot where we want them.

Battle is always sweaty work but with the heat from the acid and Rhylan's dragon fire, and the exertion of the fight, my hold on the door is getting tenuous. With each aggressive swing, I lose my grip a little more.

Still, I can't afford to stop swinging. We've got them on the retreat and, despite them continuing to spit their acid at us, our car door shields are holding up fairly well.

"Dragon, get ready to fire up the frog's legs," Dune shouts.

Rhylan's dragon lets off a guttural wail and pumps his wings to gain speed.

I've almost got the two I'm corralling pushed back when I swing, a runnel of acid runs down my forearm, and I lose my grip completely. With a curse, I watch the door sail through the air, bowling over a goblin, and leaving me completely exposed.

As another throaty hack sounds, I spin and bring up my wings to shield myself.

The hit comes hard and fast from the left and I'm knocked flying.

Someone lets off a strangled cry as I'm flapping ass over end in the air. I cartwheel until I regain my senses and start flying with intent.

With my balance recovered, I focus on the scene below and try to piece together what's happened. Someone is down and there are Elbirfae youths leaning forward in a huddle over him. They have their wings outstretched and overlapped to create a protective igloo.

Thankfully there are no more toad men in the fight.

Dune and I pushed them far enough back that Rhylan was able to fry them.

Landing with the FCO Enforcers, I pick up one of the steel sabers and start slicing through the last of the goblins. I have a sickening feeling I know who the kids are protecting in that igloo and I'm terrified to find out how bad it is.

Still, securing the mint from attack is my primary duty as a warrior.

Once that's taken care of, I can be a mate.

The last of the goblins put up no fight. I think they're trying to surrender by dropping to their knees, but no mercy is given.

This is a war they instigated and they ignored their chance to change their path.

Their deaths are swift and brutal.

When the last man falls, I drop the saber and leave Lukas's men to take care of clean up. I rush back to where Dune went down and tap the wings that are blocking me from my mate. "Enough. It's over. Let me see him."

The young warriors straighten and ease back, giving me an unhindered look at the damage done. Bile pushes at the back of my throat. "River, go to those men in black and tell them we've got a man down with severe burns."

River rushes off and I drop to my knees on the grass. "Sweet mercies, Dune. You heroic idiot. What the hell did you do?"

I don't need him to answer. We both know.

He took a hit that was meant for me.

CHAPTER TEN

Shadow

$\mathcal{I}$t's hell being the only one in the mating quint who isn't actively involved in the battles of the quadrant. It means that while the four people I care about most in the two realms are out in the world fighting the enemy, I have no idea what's happening to them.

It's nerve-racking.

The nice thing today is that I have guests to get settled. With so much to show them and explain, I can put the dangers of the moment out of my mind...at least for the moment.

"Anything you would like stocked in the kitchen just write it on the list and the brownies will take care of it through the night." I adjust Moonshade in my arm so I can point to the notepad on the counter.

"The brownies are very eager to serve and almost never seen, but they do appreciate a shiny trinket every now and then as a token of thanks."

Moonshade wriggles to be set down when we get near her water bowl, so I release her so she can drink. "We have healing milk baths and training rooms and pretty much all the same recreational games you had at Valorous Hall. Actually, very few things about Amberloq hall are different."

"It's strange that it shares the same floorplan," Terran says.

"Agreed. We all think so too. Honor was a child when her aunt moved the Amberloq force to the other location. She doesn't know what the former Guardian of the Crown was thinking, but we assume she didn't want everything to change, just to gain some distance between her and her brother."

"The sun is setting, and the warriors will be returning tired, I'm sure," Ambrose says. "Where are you thinking we should put our belongings?"

"You will all be on the second floor in the east wing. There is a lovely library and a den on the floor. It will allow you to feel like a private community even when the house fills in the next months. Come, Moonshade and I will show you."

"No need to bother," Rivka says. "You are still pale and unsteady after your spell in the vehicle. Ambrose and Terran can carry up the bags and I will fix you something to restore your strength."

"That's not necessary. You are our guest here—"

Rivka waves that away. "Nonsense. If I am living here, I am not a guest. I am honored to cook for the Desert Biome General and his mates. Please, allow me to be of service."

I honestly don't have the strength to argue, and Lukas and Honor keep telling me I have to work on my self-care, so I accept. Bowing my head, I take a seat at the table. "Gratitude. Your kindness is appreciated."

"Are they back yet?" Honor's panicked call echoes from the front entrance.

I get up to go to her, but my wolf guide has run off ahead of me. Moonshade adores Honor and tends to forget she's supposed to be my eyes when our princess is around.

With a hand on the wall, I ease around the corner and out of the kitchen and hurry forward.

I've been practicing.

There are thirty-four steps from the kitchen to the foyer. It's a straight run with no furniture for me to bump into. Counting my steps quickly in my head, I pass the first doorway that leads into the library, then the one for a powder room.

I'm almost to the main entrance when I catch up with the vision of my little wolf. She's looking up at Honor and the expression on her face makes my stomach churn. "Princess, what's wrong? Who are you frantic about?"

"Dune. Rhylan sent word to the castle security office that Dune was badly burned in the battle. He and Tundra are bringing him back, but I didn't catch where they were bringing him."

Lukas comes racing down the steps, holding one of the vials of Calli's tears we keep on hand. "Got it."

The door is still open, and a flood of excited youths come barrelling in. They're all talking over one another, and nothing can be made out.

Lukas presses his fingers into his mouth and lets off a shrill whistle. The cacophony ends abruptly. "We understand there is much to tell us. Right now, we just need to help Dune. Where are they?"

"Tundra took him to the building across the grounds," Skye says, pointing out the door.

"The milk baths," Honor says, grabbing the vial from Lukas and bolting through the crowd.

Lukas holds his hand out to me, and once we're clear of the crush of bodies at the door, we run together across the manicured lawn. The building he's taking us to houses the magical healing baths of the Amberloq.

Moonshade doesn't realize it's a dire moment and gets caught up in the excitement of the run. The rush of joy I'm getting from her is very strange when my own emotions are so fraught with worry.

"What happened to him? What kind of burns?" I can't imagine what would've burned him. The natural shielding on his wings is incredible.

"We don't know yet," Lukas says, slowing to grab the door handle to open things for us.

Moonshade runs inside and I follow, Lukas tight on our heels.

Honor is on her knees about to tip the vial into Dune's mouth.

"Wait on that a moment, babe," Lukas shouts. "We don't want the healing to kick in with his clothes merged with his skin. "We need to get him cleaned up a bit first."

Tundra is standing to the side and looks hollowed out. He's covered in blood and stripping off his weapons vest and his pants. Once he's down to his boxers, he tosses his belongings to the side before dropping into the closest milky white trough.

Rhylan has one of his claws extended and is cutting the fabric of Dune's pants to peel it away from his raw and oozing flesh. "Slecking hell, you're hamburger, my friend."

Lukas kneels to help him. "Hey, sandman. We're going to get you healed up as quickly as we can."

I wrap my arms around Honor. Her tears are falling, and I can do nothing else but try to comfort her.

Dune blinks up at us, his body trembling so badly it is more like convulsions. "That toad thing got me good, but I saved my face. I'm still sexy as hell, right?"

"Cover model material," Honor chokes.

"Nailed it. As long as..." Dune groans as Rhylan peels the pants off his left hip and takes a considerable section of his skin with him.

"I'm so sorry," the dragon says, grimacing.

"It's not your fault." Lukas frowns at Dune's state, studying the male's brilliant turquoise eyes. "Dune, listen to me. You're going into shock. I'm going to put you out so we can get things taken care of quicker."

He looks up at all of us and the panic he's been holding back floods to the foreground. "Are you sure that's a good idea? What if I don't wake up?"

Lukas reaches forward and cups his face. "I'd never let that happen. It's just a little nap and when you wake up, things will be better."

He meets Lukas's gaze and nods. "Okay, do it. I love you guys."

"We love you too, sweetie," Honor says.

Lukas presses his palm over Dune's forehead and recites something in Latin. The moment Dune's eyes roll back, and he falls slack against the floor, Lukas and Rhylan double their efforts to get his clothes off.

The damage is a horrible mash-up of fabric, blood, and sinew. Thankfully, he's not feeling it.

I turn Honor's face into my shoulder. They're at the worst of it now and are tearing more skin than they're saving.

"What did this?" Lukas asks. "He said toad thing. What does that mean?"

Tundra and Rhylan tell us of the battle against the goblins and how they had ten toad men who spit an acid venom.

"The kids warned us about the level of damage the acid would cause," Tundra says, his voice rough. "But when I ended up exposed and in the line of fire, Dune didn't hesitate."

"He's too brave for his own good," Honor says, easing back to check on things. The intake of breath as she sees the damage is nothing but a soft hiss, but it seems loud in the close quarters of the situation.

I release Honor from my embrace, bend to scoop up Moonshade, and swap the vial of phoenix tears our princess is holding for my little wolf. "How about my two girls snuggle and I'll help with Dune?"

Honor gives me a teary nod and I kiss the end of her nose. "It's almost over. He'll be fit and annoying us in no time."

"I can't wait," Honor says, sadness clouding her eyes.

I run a hand over Moonshade and then point to the men working on Dune. When she focuses on the scene, I drop to one knee and brush his matted hair back from his face. "Are you now ready for the tears to be administered?"

Instead of taking off Dune's vest, Lukas is removing the weapons from their holsters and setting them aside. "Yeah, go for it. Rhy, just yank that last bit off and be done with it. He's out and it'll heal before I wake him up."

Rhylan winces. "Okay, but it's killing me to do it. This is brutally nasty."

"Yeah, but it's gotta get worse before it gets better."

I turn my gaze to my task, not wanting to witness the brutality of what's been done to our mate.

The stopper fits tightly but after a bit of wiggling, I ease forward and dump the magical contents into his mouth. "There you are, warrior, everything you need to heal."

Lukas and Rhylan slide Dune's limp body toward Tundra and he gathers him into his arms and sinks down to submerge in the healing waters.

With everything we can do finished, I straighten, wrap my arms around Honor and Moonshade, and close my eyes. "He'll be fine now," I whisper. "We've all seen what Calli's tears can do. He'll be fine in a few hours."

And with that, Honor's tears begin to fall in earnest.

Dune

I wake to the hopeful gazes of Lukas, Honor, Tundra, and Shadow blinking above me like curious owls. Not that I mind. The depth of their concern is there, for all to see. Things are still new, and I know I was the last to get on board, but I truly do feel the love blooming between us. If I ever had any doubts about how committed they are to the screw-up of the mating group, I don't now.

I draw a deep breath, thankful my body is no longer suspended in fiery agony. "How did I turn out? Am I still extra crispy?"

Honor shakes her head. "No, sweetie, you're perfect."

I'm resting in the cradle of Tundra's arms, soaking in the healing warmth of the milk bath, and yeah, perfect sounds about right.

Except Tundra looks anything but.

Reaching up, I brush the backs of my fingers over his clenched jaw. "You okay, big man? You look more constipated than usual."

Tundra drops his forehead to touch mine and exhales. "I hate that you suffered because of me."

I cluck my tongue. "Not everything is about you, Tundra. Geez. Aren't you the one who's always telling me that?"

He chuckles and lifts his head to smile down at me. "You're right. This is all about you. How do you feel?"

"Like I'm indestructible, actually. Damn, Calli's tears are like the best pick-me-up drug ever."

Lukas pushes up from his knees and helps Honor stand. "Yeah, if the whole Fae Prima thing doesn't work for her, I'm sure she can make a killing on the black-market selling tears."

"Seriously." I draw a steadying breath and smile up at my mates. "Shadow? Do you think Phoenix tears would do anything to heal the mind fracturing of your oracle stuff?"

He blinks and looks at Lukas who seems equally bewildered.

"I don't know. It never occurred to me. I never thought of it as an injury, but I suppose damage is damage. Isn't it?"

"That's a damned good question," Lukas says. "We'll look into it. My only concern would be that the workings of oracle magic don't react the same way most of the fae magic does. We'd have to be sure we don't make things worse."

"Worse how?" Shadow says, his voice laced with frustration. "I'm blind. I'm helpless to fight the fracturing of my mind. And I can't resume my counseling practice because I might trip into prophesying and seizures in front of my patients. If Calli's tears can help, I'm willing to take the risk."

Lukas sighs. "Well, even if you're feeling reckless, that was the last of our vials. Give me some time to investigate the idea. Maybe they'll heal you, maybe they won't. We'll find out."

"Even if they hold off the decline, that would help," Honor says.

Lukas nods. "It's definitely worth a trip to the Human Realm to find out."

Honor beams. "Oh, I'm dying to spend more time with my godson and then there's the Ruic Breard development."

I give Honor and Lukas my full attention. "What Ruic Breard development? What's the news?"

Lukas shrugs. "We're not one hundred percent sure, but tonight while you guys were fighting at the mint, Creed had the foresight to have Honor scanning the city's cameras searching for Breard. He wondered about the mint being a diversion."

"And was it?" Tundra asks, looking up at our princess.

"Maybe. Using the facial recognition software, I got a hit as Ruic came out of a building and got into a conveyance owned by a Dremy Laughlin."

"A wizard," Lukas adds.

"The vehicle picked him up and drove to the Portal Hub. Except, when he stepped out of the car from the door he entered, he wasn't Ruic Breard anymore."

"What do you mean? Do you think he switched out and we lost him?"

"No. We don't think so. When I followed the vehicle using street footage, Ruic Breard was no longer in the car. And when I went back and tracked the camera footage at the Portal Hub, that man went through the Portal Gate to the Human Realm."

"That weaselly slecker. He hired the wizard to glamor him. Is he running or going after something?"

Lukas shrugs. "Yet to be determined."

Honor waggles her brows, a new light glowing in her beautiful purple eyes. "Either way, if *our* realm problem has now become *their* realm problem, we have to go get him and make things right."

Going to the Human Realm. Wow, that seems like something out of a fantasy novel.

Tales of the other realm were the stuff of myths and bedtime stories as we grew up. "Can Tundra and I come too? Even if we stay on the Pennsylvania property where there's no risk of exposure, we'd like to come. Wouldn't we?"

Tundra nods. "Definitely. I don't want to be a realm away from our mates, especially if you're taking on a snake like Ruic Breard."

Lukas tilts his head from side to side as if considering that. "I don't see why not. Sure. We'll consider it a working vacation."

"Road trip!" Honor says.

The tension of my injuries fades into the background as excitement takes its place. Good. I much prefer to see smiles on the faces of my mates.

Excitement is much better.

Tundra

By the time we get Dune back to our suite, my stomach is cannibalizing itself and I'm ravenous. And if I'm this hungry, so are my mates. With that in mind, I head down to the kitchen and—

"Tundra! Is Dune all right?" Skye rushes me as I enter the kitchen and I get my hands up to catch her before she crashes into me.

"All is well. He's back to one-hundred percent."

"One-hundred percent? How is that possible?" Terran asks. He and the other Amberloq elder, Ambrose, are sitting at the table looking confused.

Ambrose sets down his mug and frowns. "The acid of the Drexic race causes irreparable damage on contact. From what the youths described, we anticipated him being horribly maimed."

"Normally, I'm sure that's true, but Honor's best friend is the phoenix who rose to unite the realms. She keeps us stocked with vials of phoenix tears for emergencies. Once we administered them, it was just a matter of waiting for the healing to take hold."

"That's incredible," Ambrose says, though he seems more annoyed than pleased.

"Is there a problem?" I ask, ire firing in my veins.

"Apologies, Tundra, no." Ambrose raises his hands and waves away my pique. "It just struck me how many good men in our time as Amberloq deserved to be healed and saved like Dune. I am, of course, incredibly pleased for your mate."

I let his apology smooth my rough edges and stand down. "Thank you. It is a blessing, no argument, to have Calli in the family. And perhaps, having her healing available can keep the next generation of Amberloq from suffering as your comrades did."

My stomach growls and it's the kind of deep, bass rumble that turns heads.

"Oh, my," Rivka says, jumping to her feet. "You're famished, warrior. Let me dish you something to eat."

"Honestly, I came to get something to take up for Dune, but yes, I'm sure the others could eat as well."

In the next moment, Skye is rushing toward the stove and the two of them are pulling out bowls and buttering bread. Skye takes what Rivka hands her and sets up two tea trays full of food. "I'll help you carry it up to your suite."

I dip my chin. "That would be wonderful."

The two of us take the trays out to the grand staircase in the main entrance. Pushing off the marble floor, I pump my wings a few times and launch straight up the open stairway to the fourth floor.

Skye lands beside me a moment later. "Thank you for letting me come live with you, Tundra. I promise I won't be a bother."

I stop walking and turn to her. "Skye, I have known you since you were born. You have never been a bother to anyone, least of all me. You are here because you want to be, and I am thrilled to have you. As far as I'm concerned, you are family, and you belong here with me."

Even if I missed the past two years of her life, there is no doubt in my mind about who this girl is. As her smile beams up at me, I know to the depth of my soul her being here is the universe setting things right.

She and I both lost so much of our community in the past two years. Us being together is a way to heal those wounds.

"Now, enough worrying about fitting into my life. How would you like to come to the Human Realm with us and spend a couple of days with the Phoenix Quint in the Prime Palace? There is realm business to take care of as well as getting more phoenix tears and spending some time with the quint and their newborn son."

"Really? The Human Realm?" Her bright eyes bugging wide

with excitement. "Yes. I'd love that. Sweet mercies, the Human Realm."

I continue our trip toward our private suite and Skye follows. "Keep in mind, we won't be leaving the royal grounds. Fae aren't known in the other realm, so we can't go into the communities or explore because of our wings."

"Doesn't matter. I'm still going."

CHAPTER ELEVEN

Honor

"Is everyone going to be okay? It seems like bad form to invite twenty-five people to move in with us and then leave for the weekend."

Lukas chuckles, glancing into the rear-view mirror of the conveyance van we booked to shuttle us to the Portal Hub. "It's not us abandoning them. They have everything they need, Doc said he'd look in on them, and they can spend the weekend exploring the grounds and the castle."

"They'll be fine," Skye says. "Honestly, Lark wasn't wrong when she said we like having the place to ourselves. After two years of living fifty to a room, the luxury of having a bedroom to close the door, a bathroom to take a private shower, and a forest to explore without metal bars or guards watching is amazing."

"And if they have any trouble, they have enough weapons to fight off any horde of raiders," Dune says.

"Or they *would* if they had access to the armory room," Lukas says, correcting him.

"Oh, they do."

Tundra scowls over at him. "Tell me you didn't give teenagers security access to a weapon vault."

Dune scowls right back. "Of course not, frosty. You wound me with your lack of faith. I had Rhylan do a background check on Ambrose and Terran last night. We went over their Amberloq records of service. They each retired with Duty Served with Honor, so I gave them clearance to access Amberloq Hall security. They might be old, but they live by the same code we do."

"That was good thinking, sweetie," I say as our conveyance slows in front of the Dornte Portal Hub.

The vehicle stops against the curb, and we all get out and sling our backpacks and duffle bags over our shoulders. While we wait for Tundra to end our navigation tasks, Skye and I giggle at Moonshade wriggling and fighting with the leather harness and leash we put on her.

"She really doesn't like that," Skye says.

I stop watching the wolf roll around on the sidewalk and check on Shadow. "How nauseous is she making you with all that twisting and reeling around?"

Shadow licks his lips and adjusts the tinted sunglasses he's wearing to conceal his blindness. "Very. I suppose we should've been training her prior to this."

Lukas sets Shadow's hand over his elbow and makes a clicking noise to catch Moonshade's attention. "She'll get used to it. And it's only while she's a wild little pup. As soon as she's trained to stay at your side, she won't need to be bound."

Shadow nods. "I know. There are too many people moving around for her not to be lured to distraction. I couldn't bear it if she got lost or hurt."

"None of us could," I say.

Our little family group makes our way up the long front

walk and into the Dornte Hub. No matter how many times I come through here, my pride in this building remains.

Massive and round, the construction of the space has created a beautiful open atrium that rises to the glass ceiling above. It reminds me of the Roman Colosseum where the walls arch around in a giant circle and through each of the archways people are being transported to other places within the realm.

Built out of caramel and beige stone quarried from the Dornte Fringe, the walls sparkle as both sunlight and moonlight pierce four large skylights above.

It is welcoming and opulent and, as a point of first impression to the Fae Realm, I am proud Dornte shines.

No one walking through this space would ever doubt that we love and take care of our quadrant.

"I can't believe we're going through the Portal Gate and into the Human Realm," Skye says. "That seems crazy to me."

"It was even crazier coming through on the first night before any of the quadrant coordinates were set," Lukas says. "If Creed and Keyla hadn't gone missing, we never would've rushed through without more testing."

"Even I wouldn't do something so reckless," Dune says. "A dozen things could've gone wrong. It's a wonder you got through with your appendages. Man, imagine if you lost an arm or leg or even worse..."

Dune makes eyes at me and wiggles his finger in the air suggestively.

"We came through intact, as you know, but it was an uncomfortable trip. There was no helping it, though. Kotah and Doc were both about to lose their minds that Keyla up and ran away with Creed. It was a stressful time."

I can imagine. Soul Searing is rare and with it happening to two people from different realms, the shock and upset must've been incredible.

Tundra leads the way into the gate room leading to the other realm and the guard looks stunned. He straightens and brushes a hand down the front of his uniform shirt. "Princess, are you…I didn't realize you'd be traveling today."

I raise a hand. "And we'd prefer you didn't mention it. King Creed is aware we need to take care of something in the Human Realm, but it's better for the quadrant if it doesn't become public knowledge that the Guardians of the Crown are gone."

The guard dips his chin with a quick agreement. "Of course, Princess. I won't say a word." He opens a screen on his console and smiles up at me, more composed than he'd been a moment ago. "Expected duration of stay?"

"That depends on our business. A few days at most, I expect." I step around the desk and look at his console. "We're investigating a man who passed through the portal to the Human Realm. Call up the outbound footage and the traveler manifest for last night."

His hands glide across the screen with a proficiency I admire. Creed and I both worked here as teenagers, and I know how complex this system can be. Our father always said we couldn't run a quadrant if we didn't know how the quadrant was run.

He ensured we became the Jacks of all trades in Dornte.

"There, that's the man," I gesture to the footage, pointing out the man I saw exiting the conveyance last night. "What name is he traveling under?"

"Enrich Glades."

"And did he give an expected return date?"

"Three days."

"And all of his travel requirements were met?"

He pulls up the declaration file and it's marked approved. Whether he falsified the information or used magic to bluff his way through, the fact is, he gamed the system and made it to the Human Realm.

Rounding back to the traveler side of the desk, I join my mates. "We're off to find Enrich Glades."

He finishes with his screen tapping and gestures to the scanner. "Can I get everyone to scan your identities before you go through, please?"

One by one, the five of us give him our names, place our hands on the ID scanner, and wait for the red light to flip to green.

When we're all accounted for, the technician unlocks the access to the other realm.

The tunnel before us morphs from being a dead-end in twenty feet to a swirl of golden magic. The power of it tingles over my skin and when the guard gives us the signal, we begin to pass through.

I grin at Lukas and squeeze his hand. "Baby Ashborn, here we come."

~

Lukas

Remembering the first time we came through the Portal Gate is a stark contrast to the trip now. In those early hours, the moment we crossed the threshold of the rift in pursuit of Keyla, our skin crawled with the needling of a million nettles. It was truly terrible.

Then, about five yards in, the tunnel exploded into kaleidoscope colors, and it felt like we'd entered a bizarre alternate universe.

Which, I suppose, we had.

Little did I know then that my future was already being intertwined with Creed and Keyla and my path would lead me to find and fall for Honor.

The most startling contrast to the first time through and this one is the time spent traveling. Before the quadrant coordinates were established and programmed into the gate consoles, the doorways didn't line up. We had to physically cross a portion of the expanse between the two realms.

Now, it happens in the blink of a nano-second.

"Home sweet home, magic man," Honor says as we step out of the gate on the Pennsylvania property. "Are you glad to be back?"

I look around the gatehouse and search for any emotions firing up. "I don't miss the place, only the people."

"You and Hawk were accustomed to being two shrewd and powerful bachelors in a world of chaos."

I chuckle at Honor's description, but she's right. "Fast cars, expensive meals, all the best weapons to take into battle...yeah, we had a lot of good times."

"Welcome home, sir," Mallory says, standing behind his desk. "I wasn't expecting you."

I extend a hand and greet the hulderfolk male. "It's good to see you, Mallory. How are things on the home front?"

"I cannot complain. Happy wife, happy life."

I chuckle. "Agreed. We must all keep our princesses loved and content."

Honor chuckles and holds out her hand. "It's nice to meet you, Mallory."

Mallory hesitates and I see the conflict in his eyes.

Honor's brow pinches. "Is there something wrong? Have I done something to offend you?"

"Not at all, babe," I say, jumping in. "Mallory's people gain insights when they contact others. He hesitates on your behalf, to be sure he won't violate your privacy by accepting your invitation to make contact. Maybe a fist bump until you get to know him."

"Oh, that's fine. We all have our things." Honor closes her

hand into a fist and meets the man's knuckles. "Good to meet you."

I chuckle and gesture to the group. "Mallory, these are my mates, Princess Honor, Tundra, Dune, and you might remember Shadow."

Mallory nods. "I do. Welcome back, sir."

"It's good to be back," Shadow says.

"And this is Skye, Tundra's ward."

"It's a pleasure to meet you, Skye. Is this your first time in our realm, young one?"

The young lady beams. "It is. I'm very excited."

"Well, I think you'll be impressed with everything King Nakotah and his mates have accomplished."

Moonshade yips and Shadow struggles to keep a hold on her.

Mallory dips his chin. "Forgive my oversight. I forgot to welcome you, didn't I little spirit wolf?"

Shadow gets her secured in his arms. "She's a blessing beyond words but at the moment she's anxious to get her paws back on earthy ground."

Mallory chuckles and gestures toward the door. "Don't let me keep you. Please, enjoy your stay."

I consider getting into the Enrich Glades/Ruic Breard business right off the top, but decide to get everyone settled first. Moonshade is squirming and Skye doesn't need to be involved in the workings of a terrorist. Also, Hawk will be able to access all the same information when we talk to him.

I lead my crew out of the Portal Gate and into the fresh, warm spring air of Pennsylvania. "Welcome to the Human Realm, everyone. It's really not that different from the Fae Realm except the weather, the scent of the air, and the fact that fae races and magical species live unseen here."

"The air really does smell different," Dune says, drawing a deep breath into his lungs. "It's very strange."

"Does it possess a different density?" Tundra launches off the ground and does a few swoops and spins in the air before he touches down again. "No. It's the same."

"Well, lookie who's dropped in unannounced," Brant says, lumbering around the line of cabins we built for short-term stays. "Missing us, are you? Or maybe you're here to rob our realm of all the best booze? We don't have a duty-free set up yet."

I laugh. "I've got a shipment coming in for our place. If a few dozen bottles of the good stuff find their way into my packing crates, I'll risk the fine. I may know a few people in high places who can get me out of hot water."

Brant chuckles. "We'll make sure you're set up right, don't you worry. Come on. Calli's going to pee her pants when she sees you guys."

We follow Brant from the clearing where we found the portal rift and walk through the forest toward the river. Since we first were here, the quint has built a wooden bridge to span the waters below and take us to the plot of FCO-owned land where Hawk built their private residence.

In the months since they first broke ground, I have been able to get back a few times to see the construction in progress.

Nothing prepares me for the finished product.

The stone manse is both imperious and yet stylish, with lots of windows, a large, wrap-around porch out front with outdoor couches and a fireplace at the end, and ten-foot, black double doors with stained glass phoenixes blazing in welcome.

"Wow. The man outdid himself."

Brant grins. "He's a wonder. I think it's lucky for him he ended up with four mates because it increases his ability to spend money on us by four."

I laugh, but he's not wrong.

As we step into the shelter of the covered porch, a kid with freshly dyed ebony and electric blue hair gets up from playing a game system near the fireplace.

Even with the hair changed up, I recognize him. "Yarko, how are you?"

He lifts one shoulder. "Good."

"And Rowan?" Since being kidnapped by Sabastian Barron Senior, Hawk's father, Yarko has been in the care of one of the ancient Forest Lords.

"He's good, I guess. Same old thing. Living his life with his people."

I frown and meet Brant's gaze.

The bear fills us in. "The kid got bored with living with tree people. Now that the big guy is back where he belongs, it seems he's lost his wanderlust."

"But it's not his fault," Yarko says. "He's always been good to me...like really good to me."

I wave away his concern. "I'm not judging. People grow into and out of different lives all the time."

He nods, his gaze fixed on Skye.

I smile inwardly. The boy has good taste. Skye is a blonde beauty, sixteen, and has the same stunning, snowy owl white wings as Tundra.

"We'll be here for a few days working on realm business," I say, gesturing between the two of them. "Maybe you could show Skye around and tell her a bit about the realm. With her wings, she can't go into the human areas and risk exposure, but with your gift, you could show her around a few of your favorite spots?"

"Yeah, that would be fun." Yarko stands taller and smiles. "Like right now?"

"Don't be gone too long, but yeah, if Skye is game, I'm sure you'll both enjoy it."

Tundra frowns at me, so I explain. "Yarko is a friend and a

good kid. He's also got portalling abilities, so he can take Skye to have fun without the risk of exposure."

Yarko is now lighting up like a kid on Christmas morning. "I know a ton of places where fae can have fun without exposure. And yeah, we can be back for dinner."

Skye smiles up at Tundra looking tentative. "I can go, right? Lukas thinks it's okay. I'll be careful."

Tundra doesn't look convinced, but he gives in. "Of course, have fun." He takes possession of her bag and then moves his attention to Yarko. "No exposure. No place risky. And back for dinner."

"Got it. S'all good." Yarko gives him a sharp nod and then holds his hand out for Skye. "Shall we?"

The moment they disappear, Tundra looks all kinds of aggressive. I laugh and pat his shoulder. "Trust me, Iceman. I know what I'm doing. If Yarko is bored with his life and he and Skye form a friendship, maybe we can entice him to stay with us. Then we get another brave and empowered kid to mold toward the Amberloq and in the meantime, he can portal us places in emergencies."

"Brilliant," Honor says.

Brant laughs at the hostile reservation written all over Tundra's face and continues toward the front door. "I'd warn you off the boy if Lukas was wrong, but I can't. He's a great kid."

Tundra doesn't look so convinced.

I have a feeling Tundra as an older brother will be much more obsessive and protective than Skye bargained for. Oh well, the rest of us will keep him from killing people.

"Stop glowering, Iceman," I say, cupping his clenched jaw in my hand. "It's fine. Everything is fine."

And with that, Brant opens the front door of their new home and invites us in. "Hey, Calli, guess who I found over by the gate?"

~

Dune

"These are nice digs, Bear. You guys did well with this place." The two of us are sprawled out in the sunken great room of their private home, taking it all in. The leather couches, the full wall, stocked bar, the pool table. "It's a guy's wet dream. If my mates were scattered around naked and being naughty, it would be *my* wet dream."

Brant looks like a muscled behemoth of banded grizzly bear strength but is really the world's largest teddy bear. We bonded back in Dornte and I enjoy chilling with him.

We, the comedic relief, need to stick together.

"Yeah, Hawk gave us all a pad and pencil and told us to make our wish lists. Then, we whittled those ideas down into what we truly wanted versus extras and then he got on it."

"Well, you nailed it. Too bad everyone is so driven at the moment that they aren't here to enjoy it."

Brant raises his glass. "It's important to take moments to breathe and appreciate."

"This is true."

Calli took Honor to ogle the baby. Hawk took Lukas and Tundra to discuss the possibility of Ruic Breard getting through the gate with a glamor on him. And Shadow and Moonshade are taking a walk with Keyla and Kotah on the compound grounds.

"So, how does it work? You guys have your own home here and then the palace on the other side of the trees?"

Brant nods. "Yep. Kotah practically gets hives at the thought of living in a palace with everyone doting on him. Having his own place to relax with us is the grounding he needs to make this royal thing bearable for him."

"How long does he have left to serve?"

"Seven years. Then it goes to a race of elves."

"Then where will you guys end up?"

Brant shrugs and sips on the rim of his tumbler. "Who knows, maybe we'll end up on your doorstep."

"That would be welcome. I know Honor would be thrilled. So would Keyla."

I take a deep drink and sigh. "Sadly, thoughts of our future lives seem too far to focus on with everything still in the air."

"I remember that feeling. For months we traipsed all over the country trying to keep Calli safe and searching for clues on the Black Knight. There was no time to consider what our future might look like."

"But things settled down?"

Brant laughs, his deep voice filling the room. "I don't know that we're the settling down type. We've got baby Ash, Kotah is the king, and Hawk basically runs the fae world. It doesn't leave much time for settling down."

"No. I suppose not."

"So, the asshole goblin is still giving you guys trouble?"

"Actually, we think he might be here and about to give *you* guys trouble."

Brant arches a brow. "You think he got through the gate?"

"Honor's pretty sure. She tracked him getting into a vehicle with a wizard and then a while later another male stepped out and went to the Dornte Portal Hub. We've got him coming through the portal last night while we were cutting down his men in StoneHaven."

"So, what are you thinking? Is he on the run or regrouping?"

"Yet to be determined. All we know is that if he's here, he'll likely try to contact Hawk's brother. At least that's what we're hoping anyway."

"All right then, I guess we'll be taking a trip to the FCO Detainment Center in the morning."

"That's the plan. Although, Tundra and I won't be able to go with."

"That's cool. We'll leave the two of you on guard duty. You can guard our boy and we'll look for yours."

"Fine, but I don't do diapers."

CHAPTER TWELVE

Honor

"I swear he's even cuter than he was the last time I held him." With Ashborn cradled in the crook of my arm and my bestie sitting opposite me, I'm more at peace than I've been for weeks. "As much as I love our lives, I hate that we don't still live in a crappy one-room apartment together. I miss this."

"Same." Calli lifts her feet and crosses her legs underneath her on the couch. "But there are perks to the whole four husband part of our lives."

"That is very true."

I open my mouth to get into that when Jaxx's mom comes in with Ashborn's bottle.

"Here, you go, little cub." The regal blonde woman with the southern drawl hands me the milk. "He's a hungry one, our little man."

Ashborn Benjamin Jonathan Northwood Barron blinks up at me with the same bright emerald, green eyes of his mother and as soon as I brush his lips with the nipple of the bottle, he captures it with his mouth and starts suckling.

"Wow, he's serious about his bottle."

"Yep. He loves nipple, just like his fathers."

I roll my eyes and tilt my head toward Jaxx's mom. "Behave."

Calli busts up laughing. "Seriously? Maggie's been married for decades. She knows full-well what wildling men are like, don't you, Mama?"

"Thankfully, yes. Johnathan is quite the wild man himself. What fun would it be if he wasn't?" She sits on the ottoman and chuckles. "Ah, bless, look at the blush in her cheeks. You aren't one of those prim and proper princesses, are you?"

Calli laughs harder. "Oh, no. Honor is an original wild child. Remember all the trouble you got us into with boys when we were sixteen?"

My mouth drops open. "That was *you* way more often than me, and technically, I wasn't sixteen. That was only last year for me. I was an adult lying in a Traveler's bed."

Calli waves her hand in the air and flicks her fingers at me. "Don't play your mind-trippy-time-trippy games on me. My point is, whether man or beast, our mates can't get enough of our bodies."

Mama Stanton laughs. "There's that blush again."

I roll my eyes. There's no helping the flush of pink in my cheeks. That's what you get from being pasty pale and having silver hair. "Don't you two find it weird talking about ravenous men when you're talking about her son?"

Calli waves her hand in the air and flicks her fingers at me. "When did you become such a prude? Maggie was around for Jaxx as a teen, Jaxx as a bachelor, and Jaxx as a boyfriend. She knows he has sex. Hell, from what he's told me, she's walked in on him at least a dozen times."

"At least," Mama says, laughing. "He's never been one for conventional moments behind closed doors."

Calli laughs. "And he's still not."

I stare at my bestie and shake my head. "When did you become such a sexual extrovert?"

"Likely around the time, the universe bound me to four sexy mates. Have you seen my guys? How could I not be into sex with them?"

"And if she wasn't, we wouldn't have ended up with this sweet pea." Maggie brushes a caress over Ashborn's arm.

I study Jaxx's mom and feel the heat in my cheeks growing hotter by the second. "Why am I the only one embarrassed here?"

"No reason I can think of. Unless...you're not having sex with Jaxx, are you?" Calli pegs me with a look, and then they both bust up laughing.

"Oh, gimme a break. When would I have time for that? I've got my own four to contend with."

Maggie laughs and heads back toward the kitchen, waving over her head as her skirt swishes with every step. "These are not problems, ladies. Enjoy every minute of it."

Tundra

While the girls enjoy their bonding time with the baby, Hawk and Jaxx take Lukas and me to explore the communications room of their home. I expected Dune to be in here commenting on all the high-tech equipment, but he passed. I think he's still a little shaken from his injuries yesterday.

"This is damn impressive," Lukas says, standing at the raised console. "And all the FCO and royal security systems are routed through here?"

Hawk nods. "We've been bringing the systems online this week. We're almost there. We haven't played with it much, but now that you've lost your bad guy, we have a task to put to it."

Lukas and Hawk move in and get working on things. It's easy to see that they have a rhythm between them and that they both thrive on it.

"They are somethin' to watch when they're in action, aren't they?" Jaxx says, adoration in his eyes. "We all work well with him, but there's somethin' about the two of them that just makes him shine."

"It's nice they have such a solid foundation of friendship."

"It is." Jaxx points over to another machine and I take a look at what he's showing me. "We have the gatehouse completely wired and recorded so all the video and sound feeds come here to be stored."

He pulls up yesterday, early evening, and the group of seven people--five men and three women--who came through at that time. "Which one of these men do you think is your glamored goblin?"

I retrieve my tablet from the pocket of my pants and call up the image Honor forwarded to us. It was taken in the dark of night and has been enlarged to the point that it's a bit grainy, but it's not difficult to pinpoint which of them he is.

Jaxx hovers his finger over the screen and a box appears around the man's face. Tapping the monitor's surface, he selects the man we believe to be Ruic Breard and that opens up an information page in a new window. "Enrich Glades."

He taps on a number in the top, right corner of the screen, checks the information, and frowns.

"What's wrong?" I ask.

"Well, either the wizard in the car glamored your guy *and* gave him the retinal and fingerprint markers of a real business-man. Or your bad guy came through the gate six times in the last month."

Six times? "I don't suppose he'd be able to assume someone's identity numerous times with neither our system nor yours picking up on the deception."

Jaxx meets my gaze. "Me either. That leaves us with Breard assuming a fake identity and coming here multiple times himself."

"I don't like the sound of that."

Jaxx runs his fingers through his hair and shakes his head. "No. Me either."

"What's got you two looking so pensive over here?" Lukas asks, joining us.

Jaxx and I take a moment to catch them up on what we suspect and Hawk frowns. "All right, you two work on tracking Enrich Glades from last night, and Jaxx and I will go back through the records and see if we can find out anything about the previous times through. If it's been Ruic all along, we need to find out where he goes and what he does while he's here."

"Agreed," Lukas says, taking over the console as Jaxx heads off with Hawk.

"It'll take us a bit of time," Jaxx says, signing off his console. "As I mentioned this system is in transition. We haven't uploaded all the backups yet from the Portal Gate. If you need us, we'll be there, going through the footage."

Lukas gives them a nod. "Sounds good. If you don't hear from us before, we'll regroup and fill each other in at dinner at six. Sound good?"

Hawk checks his watch and nods. "Sounds about right. Good luck."

The two of them strike off and when the door clicks behind them, I step back and watch Lukas work. The male has impressed me countless times in countless ways but there's nothing quite so sexy to me than a man who is not only a competent warrior but a truly skilled intellectual.

"Why are you looking at me like that?" Lukas says, smirking at me as his fingers slide over the screen of the terminal he's working on.

"I was just thinking there is nothing quite as stimulating to me as an intelligent man who excels at his tasks."

He chuckles, pausing his work for a moment to arch a brow. "Stimulating, huh? So, is that your way of saying you love me for my mind?"

"It is...although, that doesn't discount your fine, muscled form, or your accent, or your skills wielding your weapon."

He barks a laugh and steps away from the console to face me. "I hope when you say wielding my weapon you mean my cock. And if you are, thank you for noticing. I take pride in that particular skill set."

Warmth rushes to my cheeks as my blood begins to pump harder and my pants grow tighter. I take a few, slow steps to close the distance between us and set my hands on his hips. "I always notice your cock."

"Well, well...if I didn't know better, I'd say my uber-professional, super-serious mate is flirting with me on the job. Aren't we supposed to be working in here, Iceman?"

I straighten and realize the truth of his words. "Of course. Apologies...I only meant—"

"—Oh, don't apologize," Lukas says, not letting me step back. "Things were just getting interesting. Although, getting our fuck on in the middle of Hawk's new control room might be in bad taste."

He takes my hand and tugs me toward a frosted glass door on the far wall. When we step inside, he shuts off the lights, calls a magical ball of flame to the palm of his hand, and tosses the illumination into a decorative glass vase on the countertop of the bar.

The flicker of the magical illumination refracts through the cut glass, sending prisms of golden light around the meeting room.

"This will do nicely." He shuts us in together and locks the door both with the latch and then with magic.

I glance around the room and the reality of what he's doing sinks in. "What? Here?"

He steps in front of me and flips the metal pin free from my belt. "We've been dancing around our schedules for days, trying to find a private moment. This is as good as any."

"But we were tasked with finding out where Breard went when he left the Portal Gate. Shouldn't we focus on that?"

"That's the beauty of computer tracking programs, mate. Once I plug in the parameters, the computers and surveillance feeds do the rest. And the best part is that it takes time before those searches come back."

He finishes with my belt and shoves my pants down my thighs. The clothes pool around my ankles, trapped by my boots. Dropping to one knee, he leans forward and takes my half-stiff cock into his mouth.

I groan and grip the back of his head.

The heat of his mouth is delicious, and after a few ardent moments of Lukas exercising his skills, I have to reach for the wall to steady myself.

"Mmm," he mumbles around my erection. "Hello there, my friend."

Unbuckling my weapons vest at both sides, I slide it over my head and set it on the conference table. "It hasn't escaped my attention that you are entirely too covered up."

He chuckles and the vibration around my cock is wonderful. Drawing back, his mouth pops off my crown with a wet suction and he rises in front of me. "We should do something about that."

"Absolutely." My fingers go for the waistband of his black jeans and a moment later, I've accessed the front of his pants. His body is hard and eager, the tip of his erection waiting for me to greet him.

It's both heartwarming and sexually gratifying to see how ready Lukas is for me. With Dune, there was always a level of push and pull when we got together. It was less about a desire to be loving with one another as it was just an absolute meltdown of control.

With Lukas it's different.

With him, it's passion and hunger and him wanting to pleasure me and have me pleasure him however our moods may strike us.

Lukas shifts his upper body as I kneel and unbuckle his boots and then mine. Getting off our boots means we can get rid of our pants as well.

It doesn't take us long to be naked and standing toe-to-toe. Reaching to the side, I pick up his gun and shoulder holster and hold it out for him. "Will you wear this for me?"

He grins. "Naked except for my gun, I like it. Whatever turns your crank. How about you flare your wings for me?"

I do as he asks and his cock weeps pre-cum as he groans. "They are so fucking sexy. I think I could lose it just with you naked and coming at me with those fuckers up and looking like that."

I knew he admired my wings, but I never realized they were such a sexual trigger for him.

I know now.

Stepping forward, I back him against the meeting table and claim his kiss. Mouth-to-mouth. Chest-to-chest. Thighs-to-thighs. The friction of skin-on-skin sends heat pulsing through my veins and makes my heart pound.

His tongue sweeps the seam of my mouth and I let him in. Playful and demanding, he teases and taunts. I reach between us, gripping both our cocks in my one hand and stroke tip to root.

My grip is tight, but he doesn't seem to mind.

Arching his hips into my hold, he plants his palms on the table and throws his shoulders back. "You wind me up so good, T."

He's got that backward, but who has the time to argue? Strong strokes build the intensity between us.

Lukas has his eyes closed and is getting off on me stroking him up and down his length. His chest rises and falls with each breath, quickening until he's almost panting.

It's erotically empowering to affect him so profoundly. This is more than finding physical pleasure.

This is two males loving one another.

"Open your eyes," I say, the need for his submission ringing deep in my voice.

His eyes open and I bring my wings up and flare them wide behind my shoulders. Releasing my erection from the stroking, I focus solely on palming him. "I'm going to wring you out and then use your cum to slick my cock and drive deep inside you."

He swallows and his pupils flare. "Fuck, yes."

"Tell me you want that."

He pants, his abdominal muscles flexing. "I do. So much."

I'm not usually the demanding one with Lukas, but this is the moment that changes. I want to wring him out. I want to penetrate him and brand him with the heat of my desire.

His breathing picks up and I flex my wings, stroking him off with a punishing rhythm. "Cream yourself for me. I need your release and I'm impatient to get at you. My cock is throbbing to hammer inside you."

"Fuck, yes." Lukas groans as his head tilts back and he grunts. The veins in his neck grow tight with the strain as his breath comes out in labored pants. "I'm going to come so hard."

My arm is aching with the strain, but there's no way I'm going to slow down now. "I want everything you've got."

Lukas's hips stiffen and then streams of warm cum spew out of him in silky ropes. I tighten my grip, squeezing him through his release, milking him for every ounce of his pleasure.

When the convulsions of his orgasm slow, I release his softening cock, scoop my hand over his belly, and take all that wonderful warm mess to use. "Lay back on the table and lift your knees."

Without hesitation, Lukas does as I demand. I utilize the access to his ass and slick things up. After I've got him good and lubricated, I cover my cock with the sticky smear and lean over him.

"Hold onto my wings and brace yourself. I'm not going to be gentle."

Something wild flares in Lukas's eyes as he grips the leading edges of my wings. "Alrighty then. Give me all you've got."

Despite my warning, I ensure his body accepts me inch by inch before I start to pump. Then, when I'm buried deep and my hips press against the flesh of his thighs, I watch as his cock begins to stiffen again.

Pulling him to the edge of the table, I maximize my leverage and lean into the back of his thighs. The squeeze on my erection as it slides and glides is exquisite. I close my eyes and breathe deeply. The scent of his arousal makes every cell in my body ignite.

I withdraw in a sensuous retreat and impale myself in the depths of his heat.

Once...again...and again, picking up speed.

My hunger for him is a fire deep in my balls, a glorious burn, an incredible pressure building to what is going to be a life-altering release.

But not yet. No. I'm just getting started.

Sweet mercies...I'm making love to my mate.

It doesn't get any better than this.

CHAPTER THIRTEEN

Lukas

The time-out I took with Tundra was a much-needed retreat from our busy lives. True, I may have down-played the importance of actively working on tracking our goblin fugitive, but I don't care.

I can quickly make up for the delay after we get ourselves cleaned up and get our heads back in the game.

Or I could have if Jaxx and Hawk weren't already out there taking care of it for us.

"Huh, you're back," I say, taking extra time to adjust my gun holster so I don't have to meet their teasing gazes. "I guess we didn't hear you come in."

"How could you over the throaty throes of orgasm?" Hawk is obviously amused. He takes a long draw on one of his special blend cigarettes and then opens the credenza on the sidewall. When he straightens, he tosses me a package of antiseptic wipes. "That's my new furniture. Go apologize to it."

I catch the package and toss it to Tundra, who's just coming out of the meeting room. "We've been caught in the act, T. Our penance is clean and sanitize duty."

Tundra looks mortified but opts to take the out and go clean the table instead of commenting.

"Be nice." I peg both of them with a look when it's just us. I reach for Hawk's cigarette, and he gives it up. "If you start making things uncomfortable, I'll shoot you. And might I remind you both of many moments when I stumbled in on the two of you as well as each of you with the others."

Jaxx gives me a sunny Texas cowboy smile and laughs. "S'all good, my man. We're just glad to see your quint is gelling."

Hawk nods. "See it. Hear it. Smell it."

I leave the magical cigarette between my lips and reach for the grip of my gun. I flick the strap snap free and make like I'm about to draw my weapon. "Don't say I didn't warn you."

They both bust-up.

Hawk shakes his head and pulls out another hand-rolled bundle of bliss. "I'm just saying the two of you have come a long way from you trying to shoot him out of the air while he tried to claw you to ribbons."

It's funny what our selective memory chooses to release. I haven't thought about our first encounter in ages. "Well, thankfully he's bulletproof and I didn't kill him. It would've been a loss. He's a fantastic fuck."

Tundra is on his way out when I voice that opinion and turns around and leaves again.

I laugh and take another pull. "No need to hide, T. This is us. There's no use trying to be anything we're not. And it's true. You *are* a fantastic fuck."

Tundra comes out to the security office, his face a lovely shade of pink.

Jaxx eyes him up and down and lets off a long purr. "It's the wings that get me. Those are hella sexy."

"Preach," I say, holding up my knuckles for a bump.

Tundra runs his long fingers through his ebony hair and ignores us both, striding over to look at the console screen Hawk's working on. "Have you found anything interesting?"

Jaxx and I chuckle but decide to put the man out of his misery. Stepping over to join them at the console, I offer the party favor to my mate. "It's a wonderful Turkish blend of tobacco laced with some happy oils and a dried plant that makes all the tensions in your life melt away."

"But you're still fully aware and your cognitive function is not impaired," Hawk adds. "I promise. It's taken me decades to get it just right."

I take another drag and exhale a cloud of blue-gray smoke. "It's perfection."

Tundra looks wary but joins us in a pre-dinner smoke. He pulls a breath in and the heater flares. I swear the effect is instant on him. His shoulders relax and the intense look that always worries his expression eases. "Wow, that is lovely."

"You're welcome," Hawk says, grinning. He hands Jaxx his newly lit cigarette and gets back to our quest to find the goblin. "With the information Jaxx and I retrieved from the gatehouse, we can safely say Ruic Breard has made at least eight trips to this realm since we opened for public travel."

"Well, fuck," I say.

Hawk nods. "Well said. Unfortunately, your theory about him contacting my brother hasn't panned out. I called the detainment center twenty minutes ago and no one has tried to access him today or on any of the other occasions we track him in this realm."

"But you tucked him away just in case."

Hawk grins. "You know me so well."

"What about tracking Breard's movement beyond his arrival?" Tundra asks. "Since this property is remote, I assume you have a portal station which connects to other places within your realm."

"You assume correctly," Hawk says, pulling up the next screens. "He took the portal that leads to the Prime Palace in Kansas and then he took the shuttle to the Bastion."

"The Bastion?" And just like that, all my chill is gone. "What business does he have there?"

"What's the Bastion?" Tundra asks.

"It's the central hub of fae races in the Human Realm, the heart of the fae community, laws, and government. People come and go often, so there are cabins to rent and lodges for meetings, and pretty much anything you'd need to meet and greet."

"And apparently, Ruic Breard's been meeting and greeting someone for the past month," Jaxx says.

"Or several someones," I add.

Hawk frowns and shuts things down. "Any way you look at it, we need to get there and find out what's going on."

～

Honor

The boys come back from their info gathering and even from the Great Room, I can tell they're anxious and fired up. I hand the baby to Keyla and get up to meet them. "What is it? What did you find out?"

Lukas comes in and kisses my cheek. "You were right about Ruic Breard coming to this realm. He's been here multiple times over the past five weeks and then, from here, he's been portaling to Kansas."

"To the Palace?" Keyla asks.

"No, to the Bastion," he says.

"What's the Bastion?" Dune asks, joining us.

Lukas goes on to explain that it's the political center for the fae people of the Human Realm. It's a one-stop for the fae political and legal system and the place where decisions and alliances are made.

"What kind of business do you think he's meeting about?" I ask.

Lukas scowls. "We don't know. It could be related to Breard Industries, the rebellion against your brother, expansion into this realm, or something totally unrelated."

"We'd have to know who he's meeting to know for sure," Calli says. "If it's about his company that's one thing. If it's about locking in support for the rebellion, that's something else entirely."

"If only we had connections in the hierarchy of the realm so we could find out," Jaxx says, grinning.

Hawk nods. "Where's Kotah? I think he and I need to get involved in this and find out what we're dealing with."

Keyla gets up and sets baby Ashborn into his bassinet next to the arm of the sofa. "He's in the library with Shadow. They're working on advanced meditation techniques. I'll get him."

Brant nods, pulling out his phone. "I'll text Yarko and tell him we need a means of transport. He'll be faster than us portaling and catching a shuttle."

Keyla hurries off and I glance around the room. "I guess the staycation part of this visit is over. Back to the reality."

Calli nods. "I'll get changed and pack a bag with some spare fireproof clothes just in case."

"You're coming?" I ask.

"Hells yeah. If there's a chance of battle where I can torch bad guys, I'm there. Maggie has the baby covered and there's enough milk expressed for him for his bottles. This place is practically one giant panic room, so there are no worries there."

"Still, we'll be here to watch over him," Jonathan Stanton says, draping an arm over Maggie's shoulder.

"You'll have Shadow, Skye, and Yarko too," Lukas says. "We'll send the kid straight back as soon as we get where we're going."

Calli rushes off and I point toward the foyer. "I'll get ready and meet you all at the front door."

Hawk mock-punches Lukas in the shoulder. "Glad to have you home, my friend."

Lukas chuckles. "Glad our problems keep you amused."

Shadow

When Keyla knocks and comes into the library, I sense the excitement in the air. Well, perhaps excitement is the wrong word, but there is definitely the energy of things unfolding.

"Sorry to interrupt. Kotah, we need you. There's something going on with the leader of the rebellion in Dornte. He's been meeting someone at the Bastion and is there now."

The wolf king rises from where he's kneeling in front of me and nods. "Apologies, Shadow. Duty calls, I'm afraid."

"Of course, majesty. Thank you for the time we had. It was a wonderful respite."

He extends a hand to me and pulls me to my feet. "It's not majesty to you, remember? I'm family, so I'm just Kotah. We've been over that before."

"I remember."

Moonshade rises to her feet, and I scoop her into my arms to carry her out. She's sending me images of the outdoors and her hopes that we might be heading out for a walk.

"Yes, little one, I'll take you outside as soon as we see what's going on with everyone else."

We meet Honor coming out of the powder room in the front hall and she bursts into smiles. "Hey there, how did your meditation with Kotah go?"

"It was really good. His healing energy is remarkable. I feel strong."

"Excellent. You, Skye, and Yarko are on Ashborn duty until we get back. In truth, Jaxx's parents have everything covered on that front, but you guys will be here to help if anything happens."

I appreciate her including me in the 'here to help' part of that sentence even though we both know I'm of little use to anyone.

Even if I don't have seizures or pass out, I'm blind and dependant on a wolf pup for everything I see.

I refuse to let the weight of that reality undo all the good Kotah just accomplished and lock my frustrations away. I am grateful for my life and my mates and my friends.

Smiling up at her, I try to project only gratitude and calm. "We'll be fine, princess. Go be the amazing Guardian of the Crown you were born to be."

"Be well, mate," Lukas says, lifting my chin to kiss me good-bye. "We'll keep you posted."

"Safe home. All of you," I say.

Honor cups my cheeks and presses a warm kiss on my lips. "We'll be back soon. Love you."

Tundra squeezes my shoulder as he passes.

Dune stops to talk. "Are you good if we leave? I can hang back with you, if you need one of us. I don't want us all to be gone if you have another spell like yesterday."

I squeeze his hand and lift my chin. "That is both thoughtful and sweet, but I shall be fine. Go be a warrior. I'm sure you have hostilities toward the man after what you suffered yesterday."

"I do, but still, I'd choose you."

"Oh, my heart," Honor says. "You just melt me sometimes, guys. Seriously."

Lukas chuckles. "We can melt in the privacy of our room later. Now it's go-time."

And with that, my mates go off to fight the monsters of the world and I'm left behind...again.

CHAPTER FOURTEEN

Lukas

*Y*arko flashes the ten of us to the Bastion compound and we fan out to find our goblin rebel. We need to not only locate him but also figure out what he's up to and with whom.

Hawk and Kotah strike off toward the council buildings to see if there is something on the dockets.

Calli and Honor take Keyla for a walk through the cabins. Goblins have a distinct smell and Keyla was attacked by Ruic's men when this all began. Being a wolf, she and Kotah have the keenest sense of smell. If there's a goblin here, even if glamored, she'll find him.

Jaxx, Brant, and Tundra go to search the main grounds.

And Dune and I head straight to the concierge desk in the main lodge to see who's on duty.

"You really get off on stuff like this, don't you?" Dune asks once we've got everyone sorted out and off on their tasks.

"I do. Tactical logistics is my sweet spot. Hawk's too. That's why we've always made such a good team."

"Well, it looks good on you."

I cast a sideways glance at our desert nomad and take a moment to really see him.

The sun is dropping low on the horizon and the golden light warms the sandy blond of Dune's hair. With his sexy copper skin and his beige and brown falcon wings, he looks like a mythical sun god.

My emotional pull to him grows stronger by the day and it's that connection that tells me that even as stunning as he is, all is not right.

"What is it, D? What's weighing on you?"

He meets my gaze and I sink a little deeper into those bright, turquoise eyes of his. "What makes you think there's anything wrong? I'm good."

"No, you're not. You opted out of the chase this afternoon with Tundra and me. You offered to stay behind with Shadow tonight. And you're being super sweet and sensitive."

He chuckles. "Is that wrong? I thought you wanted me to work on my sensitivity."

"I'm not complaining. I want to make sure last night didn't break you somehow."

I expect Dune to brush me off with some kind of smart-ass remark, but he surprises me yet again. "Just trying to find the balance, you know? As an Elbirfae, I've always considered myself relatively indestructible. But yesterday really hurt me... even more than getting staked to a concrete wall by a missile. And then there was Shadow's seizure. I didn't like seeing him go down like that."

"None of us did."

"Right, I know. It's just...seeing the Elbirfae survivors and hearing their stories and knowing everything that's been going on with us, it struck home how tenuous things are, you know? I never saw life as being fragile before but now it's unsettling."

I close the distance between us and wrap him in a hug. "I'm so fucking impressed by you right now, I can't even tell you."

He accepts the hug, but when I ease back, I see how confused he is.

Leaning in, I brush my lips with his in a simple pledge of my affection. "What you're feeling is the protective worries of love and empathy. Yes, life and love are fragile but that's why we band together. As a unit, we can protect not only ourselves but each other. And if you're feeling a little shaky right now, that's perfectly fine."

"Not really. We're supposed to be warriors with our mindset locked on taking on Ruic Breard."

"What makes you think that warriors can't worry for their loved ones and feel off-balance after an injury like you suffered?"

"Valorous always drilled it into us that it's a weakness to let emotions in."

I shake my head. "Valorous was wrong on more than one front. It's not a weakness to worry that your mates are vulnerable or that the innocents you care about suffered at the hands of bad men. It's a strength. It gives you the motivation and the drive to make sure that doesn't happen again."

He nods at a couple passing by on their way to the lodge. I doubt anyone in this realm even knows what Elbirfae are. He's drawing attention.

I squeeze his hand and offer him as much reassurance as I can. "Shadow isn't the only one in a state of transformation. We're all adjusting to our new lives. I, for one, am proud of the strides you've made in the past weeks. You're rocking this, Dune. Seriously."

Drawing a deep breath, he stands straighter and lifts his chin. "Thanks. I needed to hear that."

I cup his jaw and wink. "Anytime and any place, mate. I've got you."

Dune leans in and kisses me. It isn't the usual lusty meeting of mouths I'm used to with him. It's tender and laced with the vulnerability of a lover. When he pulls back, his gaze looks almost panicked.

I give him a quick kiss of reassurance in return. "Thank you for trusting me with the real you. The kiss was lovely. Now, how about we go inside and find our bad guy?"

"Yeah. Let's do that."

Tundra

Jaxx, Brant, and I travel to the northern boundary of the Bastion compound to begin our search. Jaxx and Brant both shift into their wildling forms and run through the forested area as their jaguar and grizzly bear and I fly overhead, keeping them both in sight while scanning from above.

Lukas was right when he said the Human Realm really isn't that different from our realm. Well, of the two places I've seen so far...which were both places where the fae reside. How different could they be?

The spring air is chilly and damp but the depths of the greens in the landscape are beautiful—at least those I can still see as night begins to settle.

By my estimation, we have another forty-five minutes before full dark takes over and the moon claims the night sky.

The warriors below bank right and we change course and go east along the back forest and along a massive, decorative pond. There are a dozen couples and young families walking along the waterfront trail, but none of them are Ruic Breard in his goblin form or in the visage of the glamored man.

What could he be doing here?

Lukas mentioned it could be something as benign as expansion plans for Breard Industries, but I don't think so. My instincts tell me he's not accustomed to losing and we've been able to shut him down and dash his chances to take over the right to govern Dornte.

Even better, he lost his place controlling the economic industry of the quadrant.

I doubt he's taking that in stride.

I flap my wings a few times and catch more than a few people on the ground pointing up at me. That's one difference between the realms, I suppose. Elbirfae are common enough in the Fae Realm that no one stops to stare.

Banking right a second time, we're now headed south and are passing over an extensive cluster of log cabins. Built in a rustic style and ranging in all sizes, the rental accommodations are tucked discreetly among the trees.

I pay special attention while scanning the grounds below now, looking for Honor, Calli, and Keyla. When the teams were first divvied up, I almost suggested one of the men go with the ladies but thought better of it.

Honor is a smart woman and skilled warrior, Calli is the fiery phoenix of legend, and from what I've heard from Rhylan and Creed, Keyla is both a cunning wolf and a skilled fighter.

There's no reason to think the three of them would need any help when tracking down and possibly confronting a man like Ruic Breard.

We make our final course adjustment and head west toward our starting point next to the main lodge.

My mind wanders to Lukas and Dune.

After this afternoon, I thought Lukas might choose me to partner with for the searching of the property. The fact that he chose Dune didn't bother me so much as spark my curiosity.

Lukas and Dune have always been the least agreeable to one another.

So, Lukas choosing him either had to do with building their

mating bond or wanting to oversee him or some other strategic reason I'm missing.

It's funny. I kind of considered Dune mine coming into this bonding. Sure, he's been building a relationship with Honor, but he hasn't been overly close with Lukas or Shadow.

Maybe Lukas wants to change that.

I think about the two of them alone together and wonder how that's going to work. They're both such different men.

I wonder if maybe my doubts are rooted in jealousy. Searching my emotions, I don't like what I come up with. Dune isn't just my dirty little secret anymore. He's part of this mating and it's good that the others are welcoming him into their lives.

Dune is doing so well on his personal growth.

It's astounding to see him being caring and considerate to Shadow, Honor, and the others.

No, it's not him who needs to evolve in this scenario—it's me.

I need to embrace Lukas, Shadow, and Honor seeing in Dune what I always hoped was there. He hid it deep beneath ego and sass, but eventually, I found a compassionate, brave lover we can be proud to give our heart to.

When we're back to our starting position, Jaxx and Brant slow their run and flip back into their human forms. I drop down to land with them.

"Well, other than a good, long run that didn't give us anything," Brant says.

Lukas and Dune exit the main lodge and jog over to us. When they get to where we're standing, Lukas points and doesn't stop. "Walk with us."

We fall into step, the five of us heading back the way we just came.

"Did you find something?" Jaxx asks.

Lukas nods and taps the comm earpiece he's wearing. "According to the front desk at the main lodge, Ruic Breard rented one of the large cabins on Whispering Pines Walkway. As well, he arranged for a catering package for ten which is currently being served."

"Ten?" Jaxx says, frowning. "That's more people involved in whatever this is than I expected."

"We're in position now," Honor says, over our earpieces. "Keyla had us closing in before the update. Girls get the point."

Lukas chuckles. "Fine. The girls can have the point, just don't engage until we get there. We don't know what this is about yet or who's involved."

"Not quite true," Hawk says, coming online next. "According to the docket, Ruic Breard, a goblin of the fae realm, brought the Fae Council an arcane Law of Leadership petition a few weeks back and has been schmoozing the authorities here to back his motion."

"His motion for what?" Keyla asks. "And what's the Law of Leadership?"

"You won't like it, little sister," Kotah says.

"Tell me."

"According to the woman at the clerk's office, the Law of Leadership states that in the event a fae-led realm, state, or quadrant is crippled by a fragmented government with civil unrest, someone of standing may be appointed Grand Governor to unify that quadrant and restore order."

"Unify the quadrant? He's the *cause* of the civil unrest. That's insanity."

"Unfortunately, it's not," Hawk says, the sound of his breath coming out in heavy gusts as if he's running. "He brought over countless documents proving Dornte is in a state of civil unrest."

"Because of *him!*" she shouts. "How can he cause the trouble and then be appointed to fix it?"

"It's not right," Kotah says, "but he has documentation

proving Dornte invaded a private settlement in the Travon Traverse and engaged in an unprovoked military strike."

"*Unprovoked?* They kidnapped Rhylan and were about to execute him. Creed was escorted by the Prince of Travon. It was sanctioned."

"He failed to mention that."

"Of course, he did."

We arrive at their position and find Keyla storming in a circuit of pacing. Her eyes are glowing gold, and I wouldn't be surprised if it's taking all she has not to lose control of her wolf and jump through the window of the cabin to tear his throat out.

"He's not going to get away with this," Honor says, trying to calm her sister-in-law. "There's no way."

Kotah and Hawk arrive and the two of them look more furious than winded.

Keyla looks up at her brother, her fists clenched at her sides. "Tell me this is a steaming pile of horseshit and there's no way he can do it."

Kotah frowns. "It's too soon to say anything. As a king, I'm bound by laws. We need to get in there and find out what's been said and how the laws view his claims."

"His claims are gaslighting propaganda."

Kotah nods. "I understand that—you know I do—but that does us no good at the moment."

Hawk pulls out his phone and dials for someone. "Jayne, listen. The Fae Realm is in the middle of a fucking coup. I need our legal team focused on the Law of Leadership and how we negate it. And if it helps, we're very willing to kill the man putting forth the petition. Good. Get back to me."

Honor

My entire body is vibrating with fury. Law of Leadership? Seriously? I study the exterior of the cabin in the distance. "I'm good with the killing him plan. We storm in there, slice his head off, and pike him as a warning to any other assholes with big ideas."

Keyla nods. "It's better to ask forgiveness than permission, right?"

All eyes fall on me, and I know they're tempted. "He's wanted in our realm as the leader of a violent rebellion. Every life lost in his attacks is on his head. We have every right to eliminate him."

Lukas and Hawk share a look and then Lukas shakes his head. "I would love nothing more than to agree with you on that, babe, but you're in realm politics now. Legal isn't necessarily justice."

"I can't see how it's legal for him to be in there schmoozing strangers and tipping the scales to take control over our quadrant."

"It's not," Keyla snaps. "It can't be. He's likely found some ancient loophole from centuries ago and is twisting it for his benefit."

"That might be true," Hawk says, "but until we know for sure, or what damage he's already done, or who's listening to his lies, we can't just end him."

"No matter how much we want to," I say.

"And we *really* want to," Keyla agrees.

Kotah nods. "So, since we didn't get an invitation, I say we crash this dinner party and see what we're dealing with. Maybe it hasn't gotten too far and he's just in there with a room full of fae lawyers. If that's the case, between me being the king of this realm and Keyla being the Queen of Dornte, we'll discredit the man and set them straight."

Keyla nods. "And *then* we kill him."

How did I ever dislike her and peg her as a weakness for Creed? I must've been out of my mind.

Lukas meets my gaze. "You are the Guardian of the Crown. Let's get you in there so you can guard it."

I straighten to my full height, take off my jacket, and release my wings. "And if these lawyers know what's good for them, they'll know who to side with."

"The one who's not a dead man walking."

I meet Keyla's fury and smile. "I like how you think."

Taking in the gathered group, I plan our entrance. "Since there's only one entrance into the cabin, Tundra and Dune will go in first. Lukas and I will go next. Keyla and Kotah will follow us. And then Calli and her mighty quint will bring it home."

When everyone's in agreement, we make our move and close in on them between us and the asshole goblin trying to take my quadrant down.

CHAPTER FIFTEEN

Lukas

The ten of us march up to Breard's cabin and as much as I'm hoping this isn't as bad as my gut is telling me, I'm afraid it is. Did Breard just come up with this plan or has it been in the works all along? Was this what Laryssa and Sebastian Whitehouse were piecing together? Did Breard pick up the threads of their plans?

Tundra and Dune are through the door with a force of two warriors out to make a point. The door swings wildly on its hinges, banging as it hits the wall.

The guests at the table spin to address the interruption, as a dozen mercenaries standing guard reach for their guns. I flex my fingers and sweep my palms out to the room. They are frozen in place, the element of surprise working for us.

"Let's leave those guns where they are, fellas. We're the law and aren't here to harm anyone."

Whether they believe me or not, there's nothing for them to do. My immobilization spell has taken their ability to make poor decisions out of their hands.

"What is the meaning of this?" As the autocratic and imperious declaration rings in the air, I take in the faces of the people gathered.

"Well, Fuck," I hiss, pissed that once again, my instincts called it. Why do I always have to be right?

"Mother?" both Kotah and Keyla say at once.

Honor looks from them to me. The confusion in those purple irises is unfortunate. "Mother? What am I missing?"

"What's this about?" Hawk snaps, stepping in beside Calli.

I lean close to Honor and whisper in her ear. "Those aren't lawyers like we thought. That's the Fae Council and the woman in the green, silk gown is Keyla and Kotah's mother."

Honor frowns. "I don't like the sound of that."

"No. I don't suppose we should."

"Mother," Kotah says, stepping forward. "Hawk asked a question. What is this about?"

Malayna Northwood lifts her chin and remains standing at the head of the table. Leaning forward on tented fingers, she sends us an icy glare. "I don't believe our business is the concern of your entire depraved family."

Keyla gasps. "Depraved? Don't you dare speak of our family while looking down your nose at us."

"And by *us*, do you mean the three men you sleep with or are you referring to the four people your brother beds?"

"Watch your mouth." Kotah's eyes are glowing gold, a threatening growl ripping from his chest. "Or have you forgotten your place once again?"

Keyla scowls at the woman and shakes her head, her long, chestnut hair swinging to brush her hips. "She most definitely has. If you remember, Mother, I was Soul Seared and Kotah was bonded as a Guardian of the Phoenix. The wisdom of the fae universe trumps your stuck-up and prudish ideals any day of the week."

"Hush, Nakeyla. You sound like a common guttersnipe. I taught you better."

Kotah raises his hand and interrupts the family drama. "All of you sit. Get comfortable. No one is going anywhere until this is settled, except you men with your hands twitching to get to your weapons. You are dismissed."

"And who the fuck are you to order us around?" A thug standing against the far wall says.

Kotah removes the choker he wears around his neck and exposes the burgundy fretwork tattooed there. "I'm the Fae Prime of the Human Realm and your king. So, when I say you are dismissed, it's my way of telling you politely to get the fuck out."

Damn, wolf.

Hawk said Kotah has really grown into his position and he's right. And the look on Malayna's face is too priceless for words.

"Gentlemen," Calli says, stepping forward. "I believe you heard your king. And if you're still considering your odds of staying here and causing trouble, I'll introduce myself. I'm the Prima of the Human Realm, your queen, and the Fae Phoenix."

To punctuate that point, Calli walks forward, bursts into flame, and approaches them in her woman aflame form. The heat she gives off is incredible and even the toughest of the men is twisting away to shield themselves from the flames.

"You have thirty seconds to get out of this cabin and head back to the main lodge or I'm going to grab your balls and fry your boys just for the fun of it."

Brant chuckles. "I kind of hope they don't leave."

But Brant is left disappointed because they do.

When they step out, Calli returns to her previous form—with clothes for a change—and Honor points toward the door. "Dune and Tundra, please ensure the hired guns don't get any bright ideas. We don't wish to be interrupted."

"Yes, Princess," Dune says, as he and Tundra head outside.

"So, I take it this is your fugitive," Hawk says, pointing at the man sitting at the opposite end of the table from Kotah and Keyla's mother.

I step forward, calling on my source power. "That's him, though he doesn't look much like himself tonight."

Rounding the table, I set my hand on Ruic Breard's shoulder and short circuit the glamor giving him a pleasant humanoid form. As the illusion is destroyed, he returns to being a weaselly green snot of a man with a knobby nose and beady, coal-black eyes.

The Fae Council has the good sense to be alarmed.

"Your Honors, meet Ruic Breard, goblin, anarchist, and the asshole inciting the violence within the Dornte Quadrant."

"And here you all sit, eating with the most wanted criminal in the Fae Realm," Honor says. "We came to extradite him back to Dornte to face the charges mounting against him."

"But he's...you can't." Aleandi, the Grand Chancellor of the Fae Council, is incredibly tall, with a delicate, willowy frame and a powder pink tinge to her skin. Her eyes are as round as two moons and glisten, reflecting light like iridescent pearls. "We have an arrangement in place. Lord Breard has our support."

"Your support for what?" Honor asks.

Malayna sets her cloth napkin over her lap and smooths it out with a practiced hand. "To reinstate peace in the Dornte Quadrant by allowing Lord Breard to assume leadership."

Keyla gasps. "You can't be serious. You actually sat here with the man terrorizing the Dornte Quadrant and agreed to grant him ruling power over Creed's kingdom? *My mate's kingdom?* I knew losing your place as Prima was a blow to your ego, but this is nuts. You've lost your mind."

"Nakeyla, I won't have you speak to me this way. It's done. The papers are signed and filed. Lord Breard—"

"—Is not a lord," Honor shouts, stepping forward. "He's an

underhanded businessman who tried to keep our quadrant prisoner first with violence, then with threats, and now with lies.
He has no claim on Dornte and you have no right to imply he
does."

Kotah's mother seems to take offense to that and stands. "I
assure you we do. The laws which govern StoneHaven were
written a long time ago. Yes, since then, a great many fae
emigrated to the Human Realm and a war divided our two
communities, but the legal tenets remain. We have done our due
diligence and verified the Law of Leadership can be enacted."

"And you thought you'd just believe this asshole spinning
his tales of woe instead of coming to see for yourself what's
going on?" The growl of Keyla's wolf is a menacing promise of
blood about to be shed. "This isn't about reinstating peace in
Dornte. This is about you trying to control me and taking
what I value because I walked away from your psychological
games."

Kotah grips her wrist and pegs the council with a furious
glare. "It won't stand. Whatever you think you've set in place, I
will tear down. You have grossly overstepped. What in the two
realms would ever make you think you have the power to
govern the outcomes of the other realm?"

Malayna smiles. "Because while you have been so distracted
with the plight of the Fae Realm and your mud-blood offspring,
I've enacted a little legal coup of my own."

Kotah's gaze narrows on his mother. "Call my son a mud-
blood again and I'll rip your fucking throat out, you hateful
bitch."

A threatening turn curls her lips in a cold smile. "So, it's
come to this, has it? I suppose I acted just in time then."

"Acted on what? What have you done?"

She opens the folder on the table before her and offers the
top document to him. "I think, when you find the time to check,
the position of the Fae Prime has been relieved of actual power

and is now a figurehead position. All meaningful power has been transferred to the Fae Council."

"On what fucking grounds?" Hawk shouts. "I established this fucking council and at no time were any of you given the clout to do something like this."

"It's a vote of non-confidence," Kotah says, reading the paperwork before handing it back to Hawk. "It says I don't exhibit the forcible presence needed to hold the power of my throne."

"I'm sorry, Nakotah," Malayna says. "You've just never had the killer instinct."

In an explosion of chocolate and silver fur, Kotah's wolf launches through the air and vaults onto the table. The ivory of his teeth shines as he lunges for his mother and clamps his maw around her throat.

A violent twist.

A spray of blood.

An enemy taken down.

Malayna Northwood slumps back into her chair, her vacant eyes wide with panic and the rush of death.

Holy fuck! Kotah just slew his mother.

Accustomed to responding to violence with quick reflexes, even I'm at a loss.

The room erupts in a wave of panic and council members start scrambling for the door.

Kotah shifts back to his human form. Standing naked on the table, blood dripping down his chin and chest, he points to the exit. "Everyone who signed that paper dies by my hand tonight. You asked for a king with killer force...you reap what you sow."

Keyla's eyes are wide, but she doesn't hesitate. She grabs the non-confidence petition from Hawk's hand and starts reading her brother the names listed aloud.

"If you didn't sign get out of the way." Hawk gestures to the back corner of the cabin and grabs the arm of one man shuffling to join the frantic retreat. "Nice try, asshole. You signed...therefore, you die."

The councilman starts to fight back and then the world goes to hell. The screaming must've incited the return of the mercenaries because the air explodes with the *tat-tat-tat* of semi-automatic gunfire outside the cabin.

The mayhem already in progress takes a wild turn.

"Incoming! North wall!" Tundra shouts outside.

The sidewall of the cabin explodes in a detonation of wooden chunks and splinters.

I dive to get out of the way.

Building debris blankets me in a barrage of wood, metal, and drywall. I choke on the dust, spitting out the grit of dirt coating my tongue.

A sharp pitch rings in my ears as I push at the broken logs pinning me down. There's no time to catch my breath. If the mercenaries follow their handiwork, I'm down and exposed.

Groaning, I shift the heavy logs and roll to get free. The world is spinning at a dizzying pace.

Fucking hell.

Glancing toward the source of the explosion, I see the chaos of the cabin spilling out to the forest.

"Let me up," Honor says, elbowing me in the thigh. I glance down at my mate pinned beneath me and she's pissed. "I'm a warrior, remember?"

"Sorry. I didn't even realize I tackled you. Mate instinct, I guess."

"Well then, get off me, mate. I'd rather fight than be flattened by you and buried under filth."

I chuckle, rolling to the side as I unholster my Sig Sauers. Back on my feet, I take in the damage.

Wow, the entire one side of the cabin is missing, and that opening is providing a huge point of access for those angry mercenaries to get back inside.

What are our casualties?

Hawk is corralling the fae counselors who had the good sense not to go against Kotah and the Phoenix Quint. Keyla is with her brother, overseeing the slaughter. Jaxx and Brant have joined Dune and Tundra outside. They're taking on the brunt of the mercenaries. And Honor and Calli are beating back the council members trying to escape.

"Where's Breard?" I ask.

Honor looks around and frowns. "I don't know. I lost him in the explosion."

Damn it.

"Okay, I'm on Breard." I check my guns and, when I'm sure nothing got damaged in the explosion, I'm out the hole in the side of the cabin and looking around. "Dune and Tundra, in the air. Find Breard. Now."

CHAPTER SIXTEEN

Tundra

*a*s Lukas falls into a position to back up Jaxx and Brant, Dune and I launch into the air. Night has fallen and although Elbirfae vision in darkness isn't completely discounted, I'd prefer if it were still daylight.

I glance up at the night sky, hoping for some moonlight and my heart stops in my chest. The moon is blood red and it's casting a scarlet glow onto the world below. "It's the next part of Shadow's prophecy," I shout on the wind.

With the battle unfolding below us, I can't help but think this is the pivotal moment we've been waiting for.

The child of fire, the moon of light,
A sea of blood to stain the night,
The foe of freedom, the king is down,
A war of outcasts to hold the crown.

"Holy shit," Dune says, staring back at me. "Are we the outcasts to hold the crown?"

"I don't know. Maybe?" I level off my flight, circle around, and hover over the scene, searching. "Do you see Breard?"

"No."

Jaxx's jaguar and Brant's bear are racing through the trees, weaving between cabins and taking down the men shooting at them. With the council members dressed up, it's easy to pick them out and distinguish between them and the mercenaries.

It was nice of them to dress for the occasion.

Lukas is doubling around the back of one of the cabins. Honor and Calli emerge together and Calli is in a partial phoenix transformation. When she gets outside, she morphs even bigger and ignites into her full phoenix form.

Her body transforms and now she's a fifteen-foot mythical firebird with a thirty-foot wingspan. With a shrill scream, she pushes into the air and swoops through the forest.

Her grace in flight is impressive but not nearly as impressive as her accuracy with her fire breath. She has no trouble picking off mercenaries and scorching them on the spot.

When the security for hire realizes they are now fighting for their life against the phoenix, they turn their weapons on her.

In my head, I know Calli is hot enough that bullets don't reach her, and she is a warrior force.

In my heart, I hate that the female, the mate, the mother of a newborn child is being targeted.

Still, if they're wasting their ammunition on the phoenix, they aren't spraying it at my mates.

Gunfire rings off behind me and I arc back around to check on my mates. Honor has joined Lukas and the two of them have disarmed the men they're facing and they're fighting hand-to-hand.

The Wolf King and his sister launch through the open wall of the cabin, lift their noses in the air, and then tear off toward the pond.

Dune and I are still searching for any sign of Ruic Breard. With everything that happened, I understand how we could've lost him in the chaos of the explosion, but I don't understand where he disappeared to.

From our vantage point, we can see the end of the forest in all directions. If he abandons the cover of the forest and accesses the open area by the lodge, the pond, or the parking lot, we should see him.

But we don't.

Where the hell did he go?

~

Lukas

Honor and I kick the asses of another couple of men and make our way back to the cabin to see what damage is done. Hawk's inside with a frantic few members of what's left of the Fae Council.

There are five down with fatal wounds and by the way Kotah rushed out of here with his nose to the ground there will be several more before the night is through.

As we move in, the scent of foul magic singes my nostrils. Honor rubs a hand over her nose and frowns. "Is that you?"

I peg her with a look. "I'm hurt. Do you think my magic stinks?"

"It was a simple question, magic man. Don't get defensive."

I laugh, scan the scene of death, and shake my head. "It's not me. Likely one of these dead council members had a glamor that soured after their death."

"Well, they stink," she says, moving toward where Hawk kept the remaining Fae Council members sequestered. "Congratulations on being smart enough not to fuck over the Fae Prime. It looks like your next order of business is to fill quite a few empty seats."

The cutting edge to Honor's voice isn't something we hear often. I suppose having lived through a kingdom double-cross herself and knowing these are the people who gave Breard the power to take her quadrant, she's rightly pissed.

I'm not surprised to see Dane, the wildling representative in the safety zone. Wildlings are loyal and the Quint is the strongest of the wildling races. He's too smart to go against that.

DenysTa, Queen of the Pixies lives on too. She and Kotah have an arrangement that gives her a seat on the council. No use going against him. He's her invitation to this party.

I nod to Aleandi, the Grand Chancellor of the Fae Council. She has no love for any of the Northwood rulers, but I can see why she would side against Malayna. The ex-Prima thought herself to be the queen of every situation. I'm sure Aleandi won't be mourning her removal from the council.

"How about we escort these folks back to their cabins?" Hawk says, enlisting my help.

"Of course."

Aleandi shakes her head. "We can't simply go back to our homes. More than half the Fae Council has been murdered by the man who calls himself our king."

"He more than calls himself your king," Hawk snaps. "He *is* your fucking king. He's also a wildling. And how do wildling leaders retain leadership when challenged, Dane?"

The lion shifter lifts his chin. "We fight to the death."

"And is that considered murder?"

"No. It's part of the foundation of our laws. As I tried to explain to Malayna and her followers when she announced her plans, Kotah had every right to put those who challenged him to death."

"Have the complaints of the non-confidence been settled?" This time, Hawk doesn't look to Dane for the answer, his gaze lands on the Grand Chancellor.

The woman seems to have gathered herself enough to know

what's good for her and nods. "No one here shall ever again question Nakotah Northwood's ferocity as a leader or his dedication to hold his throne."

Hawk nods. "That's very wise."

"And what about Ruic Breard and his petition to gain leadership of Dornte?" Honor asks.

Aleandi shrugs. "I honestly don't know. The Law of Leadership is truly a legal avenue pursued by Lord Breard—my apologies—by the goblin, Ruic Breard, but it was Malayna who verified his claims. With her sudden and unexpected demise, I suppose we'll have to look into the matter again."

"And I'm sure you'll make the correct decision the second time," Honor says, flaring her wings. "If not, we'll be back with our king and we'll have a repeat performance of tonight's bloodshed."

Aleandi has the good sense to pale.

Keyla trots into the cabin and shifts to her female form. "I guarantee you my mother made a side agreement with Breard to take my mate's quadrant away so I would see the error of my chosen path and return to this realm to remain under her thumb. She never cared about the safety of Dornte. I'd say it's too bad that these councilors were swayed by her delusions, but there is no excuse for disloyalty, so they got what they deserved."

Honor

When the last of the gunfire dies down and Lukas and Brant escort the living Fae Council members back to their cabins, I'm left looking over the carnage of our night. "How the hell did things go so far off the rails?"

Hawk sighs. "It's the ruthless greed of power-hungry folks. It never ends well."

Kotah and Keyla's mother is the poster child for that statement.

Calli and Keyla come in to join me and I block Keyla's line of sight. "I'm so sorry for your mother's betrayal. Maybe you don't want to see her like this."

Keyla lifts her chin, the light catching on the choker of her royal status as it glistens. "Wildlings are as much animal as we are human. My wolf would've torn her throat out if Kotah's hadn't. That woman was no mother of mine."

"No, she wasn't," Calli says. "And thank the gods for that. The two of you, raised by your pack mates in North Dakota, turned out much better than you ever could have with such a selfish shrew guiding your upbringing."

Keyla steps around me and studies the carnage of her brother's rage. "Everything happens as it's meant."

Hawk pulls Keyla into his arms and kisses the top of her head. "Why don't we call Yarko, and then you ladies can head back to our place? We'll clean things up and join you when it's done."

"That's a good idea," Calli says, draping her arm across Keyla's shoulder. "Let's go hug Ash and focus on better things."

My brother's mate is a small but feisty female. As a rule, her fiery presence makes her appear larger than she is in reality. Tonight, that's not the case. Tonight, she looks like a twenty-year-old girl who's been betrayed from within her inner circle.

Hawk shifts to escort us toward the door and Keyla avoids the prompting. "One second. There's something I need first."

She approaches the body of her mother, moves a section of bloody green silk, and finds a thick platinum chain hanging free from its broken clasp.

Looking down, she bends to search under the chair and straightens holding a signet ring.

"This was my father's pack Alpha ring. When he died, it should've gone to Kotah. Mother refused to part with it. Kotah didn't want to add to her pain of losing her mate, so he never fought her, but it should be his and, in time, Ashborn's."

She holds it out for Calli to take but she shakes her head. "No, sweetie. You give it to him. The two of you need to process all this bullshit together."

Keyla closes her fingers around the ring and straightens. "Yeah, I think I'd like to go visit my nephew now."

Calli glances over to me and tilts her head toward the exit. "Are you coming with us?"

"You two go. I've got to check in with my guys and find out about Breard. We'll meet you back there in a bit."

"Do you want me to stay?" Calli asks.

"No. Take Keyla and Kotah back to clean up and relax. We'll be there as soon as we figure out where we stand on the goblin front."

"Good luck. Come home as soon as you can."

I walk them out of the cabin and glance around the forest, searching for Dune or Tundra. It's dark and without the light of the moon to guide us—

I stare up at the night sky and a chill runs down my spine. "A blood moon."

"Is that a thing?" Dune asks, landing beside me.

"It is. Twice a year in the Human Realm, a lunar eclipse makes the moon look like it's red. How bizarre is it that it's happening tonight when all this is going on? A coincidence? I think not."

"Tundra thinks it's Shadow's prophecy. *The child of fire, the moon of light, A sea of blood to stain the night, The foe of freedom, the king is down, A war of outcasts to hold the crown.*

I shiver a second time, the hair on my arms standing on end. "It's too close to the point to be a coincidence. We thought the child of fire part was complete because Ashborn is already here but what if we misread that. If the entire prophecy was about tonight, it fits."

"How so? What did we miss?" Dune looks confused and I remember he and Tundra were outside when Keyla's mother made her big reveal.

"We spent the day with Ashborn, the child of fire. The moon of light is a blood moon, as well, a sea of blood spilled to stain the night. The foe of freedom is obviously Ruic. He usurped Creed's power and at the same time, the Fae Council took Kotah's power from him. So, if Creed and Kotah are no longer in power, we become the outcasts fighting to hold the crown."

"Creed and Kotah are no longer in power?" Dune asks, looking shocked.

"They weren't, but then Kotah killed most of the Fae Council. They're rethinking their decision now."

Dune's brow pinches. "He did what now?"

I glance around and lower my voice. "We'll talk about it privately later. For now, let's focus on Ruic Breard. Where is he?"

"We don't know. We don't think he had time to run beyond the boundaries of the forest, but we can't find him. Jaxx and Brant did a full sweep of the treed area and circled all the cabins. They couldn't pick up his scent."

Lukas returns from his escorting duties and kisses my cheek. "How's everyone holding up?"

"We're trying to figure out where Ruic Breard went. We don't think he got out of the forest, and yet there's no sign of him or his scent to tell us where he went. It's like he just disappeared."

Lukas frowns at me and rolls his eyes. "Well, fuck. He didn't disappear—he teleported. Remember that stank of dark magic right after the explosion? I'd bet my left nut that was residual magic from a dark wizard's teleportation spell."

"Teleported? To where?"

Lukas shrugs. "I have no idea."

"Do you think he could make it all the way back to the Fae Realm?" Dune asks.

"No. He's here somewhere."

"Can you track the spell?" I ask.

He considers that for a moment and frowns. "Maybe if I'd seen how he disappeared or been close enough to take a read on the power surge, I could guess, but this long after it happened, there's no way I can track him."

"Well, fuck, is right," I say, groaning as I scowl up at the blood moon. "I can't believe that asshole slithered under another rock. He got away again."

Lukas presses his fingers under his tongue and whistles. Waving toward the night sky, he flags Tundra down to join us.

"Did we find Breard?" he asks.

Lukas shakes his head. "Not this time. But make no mistake, we will get our man. And when we do, we'll take a page out of Kotah's playbook and make sure he never bothers us again."

"I'm looking forward to that." I take a deep breath and fight not to scream at the night sky. "It's fine. Everything is fine. We'll find Breard and we'll end him. It just won't be tonight."

Dune looks at me and pats a hand on his abdomen. "Does this mean we can go back to the Pennsylvania compound and have some dinner? I'm famished."

I slide my arm around his back and lean against his shoulder. "Does anyone have the contact info for Yarko? We've got bellies to fill, babies to hold, and goblins to locate."

Lucas pulls out his phone and fires off a text. "Sounds like a busy night. We better get started."

CHAPTER SEVENTEEN

Shadow

*T*he first to return is the Wolf King. With the slam of a door and a wafting stench of blood and death, Kotah arrives home and heads straight up the wide staircase toward the second floor.

I would ask if everything is all right, but the answer is in his blood-soaked hair, neck, and face.

Moonshade whines and rubs against my shin asking to be picked up.

I oblige her, happy for the closeness of having her near as well as the focus of her vision. When she's on my lap, I see the world around me almost as well as if I weren't sight-impaired.

Her anxiety leaks into my mind and I stroke the top of her head and rub her ear. "I'm not sure, sweeting, but you're right, that was a lot of blood."

Skye comes into the Great Room and sits on the sofa opposite me. "How are you feeling? Tundra says you have oracle genes activating and are in a state of transition?"

I scrub my fingers through Moonshade's long fur. "I am well enough, thank you. Is everything going well with you?"

"I think so. It was a bit of a drag to get called back here, but Yarko takes his job as Quint shuttle very seriously. We'll explore the realm more once he's back."

"I'm back," Yarko says, chuckling. "No. Actually, I'm kidding. I've got another text from Lukas, so I'm just dropping off the ladies and going back on another run. BRB."

Skye chuckles as the kid flashes out and leaves us with Keyla and Calli.

"Are you all right, Princess?" I rise from the couch, taking Moonshade with me. "What's happened?"

Keyla blinks out of a haze of thought and lifts her chin. "Too much to process at the moment. If you'll excuse me, I need to check on Kotah. Is he upstairs?"

"He is. He went up about ten minutes ago." I wait until I hear the weight of her footsteps on the floor above us and lower my voice. "What happened? And more importantly, is anyone we love hurt?"

"Physically, no," Calli says. "Come with me. I want to check on the baby and I'll give everyone the quick version of what happened."

I follow Calli to the kitchen where Maggie and Jonathan Stanton are sipping tea and chatting quietly in the corner. The moment they realize Calli is back, they stand to greet her.

"Oh dear, you smell fresh from a fire." Mama takes a visual inventory of her daughter-in-law. "Things went sideways on you, did they?"

Calli smiles down at her sleeping baby and then spends the next few minutes, pulling out plates and extra cutlery. While she prepares for the return of hungry warriors, she tells us of the fallout of the evening.

When she finishes, she meets our gazes and forces a poor

attempt at a smile. "I guess your prophecy is now complete. Congrats, Shadow, you called it."

"It's nothing to be congratulated on," I say, my heart aching for Keyla and Kotah. "I wish none of this had happened."

"I know it's not kind to speak ill of the dead," Jonathan says, "but that woman didn't deserve those two kids. How she could go through life with such disregard for them is beyond me."

Calli finishes with her preparations and leans in to smell the food warming on the stove. "Exactly right, Jonathan. It's beyond all of us. And unfortunately, it'll be Kotah who suffers most for his mother's actions. Malayna's betrayal and his actions to end her will hurt him so deeply."

"You're wrong, *Chigua*." Kotah and Keyla join us from the main hall. The Wolf King is fresh from the shower and looking much more relaxed than he did twenty minutes ago. "My mother twisted me in knots my whole life. Tonight, she finally set me free. Her betrayal freed me to finally rid our lives of the cancer that has poisoned our happiness for two decades."

Keyla nods. "No longer. We will return her body to the wolves of the forest where our father was lain and that will be the end of it. May the two of them find peace with one another because they never spared any for us."

Maggie rushes across the kitchen to give each of them a hug. "You are both loved beyond measure. In this family, love conquers all."

"Damn straight," Honor says, arriving with Lukas, Dune, and Tundra. Moonshade wriggles in my arms and I set her down to run to our princess. "I didn't know your mother, so I won't pretend to understand what she put you through, but this family we're making, by blood, bonds, and by choice, is about respect, support, and love."

"And on that note," Calli says, gesturing to the pots on the stove. "We've got a lot of hungry mouths to feed. Let's refuel and then we can regroup once the rest of us get back."

"Where are the boys?" Mama asks.

Kotah picks up a plate and some cutlery. "I'm afraid I may have lost my temper and left them with quite a mess to clean up."

Lukas chuckles. "And quite a few vacancies on the Fae Council."

Calli waves that away. "They deserved it. And hey, on the bottom of the job description, we can put, Traitors, need not apply, and include a picture of their predecessors."

"I bet that will do a lot for crown loyalty," Lukas says. "Good idea."

Kotah takes a deep breath. "It once again illustrates the need for us to have an overseer on the Fae Council."

"Consider that position filled," Hawk says, striding into the room and straight for Kotah. "I'm so fucking sorry—"

"Language, dear," Maggie says, frowning.

"Sorry," Hawk says, starting again. "I'm so, deeply sorry anyone thought they had the right to usurp your leadership. I built that council with the hopes that giving a voice to the species and races would unify us, not inspire infighting and deception."

Kotah sets his empty plate back on the counter and falls into Hawk's embrace. "It's not your fault. I don't want you to take on any of my mother's manipulations as something you could've prevented. She was a hateful, selfish person and her hold on us is over."

"We should drink to that," Keyla says. "I can't be the only one who needs a drink. No, check that. I need many, many drinks."

Kotah finishes filling a plate and smiles up at his sister. "An excellent idea. I want to eat, spend some snuggle time with my son, and then I will be challenging Jaxx to keep our evening filled with drinks and entertainment."

"I accept that challenge," Jaxx says.

He and Brant join us, and our Texan cowboy has a little

extra swagger in his hips. Any prospect of a party does that to him.

They both go straight to console Kotah and then move on to Keyla. "Everyone eat up because you're going to need your strength. You know the saying. Eat, drink, and get sexy."

"That's not the saying, Jaguar," Lukas says, laughing. "But points for enthusiasm."

Jaxx waves away Lukas's correction. "Hush now. You're in our house and the quint house rules state, I make all final decisions on the party planning."

Keyla chuckles. "Hey, I don't have any mates here. How am I getting sexy?"

Jaxx winks. "Trust me, little sister. I've got you covered. There are no wallflowers at my events."

Dune

The evening unfolds and as time passes and the drinks flow, the violence and heartbreak of the night fade into the background. I have to give Kotah and Keyla credit, they aren't celebrating, but they're not consumed by the emotions of the day either.

"So, this is us," Lukas says to Tundra and me around eleven o'clock. "We're a bit of an inappropriate muddle of chaos, but we work."

"It's nice," Tundra says. "I've never had anything like this."

"Until now," he says, holding up his glass. "This is the beginning of our lives together. We've got nothing ahead of us but time to make things better."

I finish my drink and set the empty bottle on the counter. "I'm looking forward to that. Not that I have any complaints about where we are now, but I'm looking forward to really settling in."

Lukas swallows. "I think we all are. Sure, life is hectic now, but things will slow down once we get this goblin rebellion bullshit taken care of. And hey, until we get there, we'll have fun along the way."

"Dune, you don't have a drink in your hand," Jaxx says, zooming past with a pan of chicken nachos. "No empty hands at one of my parties."

"Did someone say party?" Creed says, rounding the corner from the front entrance and dropping down the one step into the sunken Great Room. "Hey, boys, looks like we got here just in time. Jaxx's nachos just came out of the oven."

Keyla turns from chatting with Calli by the fireplace and lights up as Creed, Rhylan, and Doc fill out the guest list. Jogging with her arms out, she rushes to her mates, and they wrap her in a group hug. "How are you here? Who's watching the quadrant?"

Rhylan winks. "I set Dornte on autopilot for a few hours. Our enemy is currently out of town, and we heard our girl needed us."

Doc nods, pressing a kiss to her forehead. "We heard what happened, so we locked down the land and came running."

Closing her eyes, she leans her head against Creed's chest. When her tears start, we all pretend not to notice. Her mates usher her out for some privacy but despite the emotion of the moment, everyone seems to be doing really well...considering.

"You're amazing, puss." Calli raises her mocktail as she crosses the room and zones in on the nachos.

Jaxx holds up his tumbler and blows his mate a kiss. "I said I had her covered. They can't stay long, but they'll cheer her up. This, in fact, brings us to the third part of our night. We ate. We drank. So, does anyone remember what happens next?"

"We get sexy!" Calli grins and crunches on a couple of nachos. "What have you got in store for us tonight, puss?"

"Well, kitten, I'm glad you asked..."

CHAPTER EIGHTEEN

Lukas

I close the door to our guest suite and smile at Honor sipping from a tumbler and lounging on one of the two couches in the center of the sitting room. The tray Jaxx gave us for our party favor is sitting on the coffee table and I'm more than a little afraid to dive into it.

Jaxx is an amazing man, but the jaguars seem to have fewer boundaries and filters than many of the other wildling races. Their animal sides are more playful by nature and therefore less inhibited.

"Is everyone sorted?" Honor asks.

"Almost. Tundra wanted to check in with Skye. She and Yarko are playing video games in the recreation room, and he wanted to make sure she doesn't stay up too late."

"Yes, dad," she says laughing.

She's not wrong. Tundra is going to be a rigid guardian. Thankfully, Skye doesn't seem to mind.

"Dune is doing a perimeter check with Shadow and Moonshade, and when our little wolf has had her run and is set for the evening, they'll be up to join us."

"Excellent."

I free the buttons of my shirt and untuck the tails from my jeans. "And now that everyone is in for the night, we can focus on unwinding. Do you want to play Jaxx's game, or would you rather have a massage, a soak in the tub, or a cuddle by the fire?"

"Mmm, as lovely as a night with the five of us in front of the fire sounds, Jaxx went to all the preparation of coming up with this game. It would be a shame to disappoint him in the morning when he asks how we enjoyed it."

I chuckle. "All right, perfect. Why don't you take your turn in the washroom now and when the others arrive, we'll be good to go."

I hold my hand out to help her off the couch. When she's on her feet, I tilt my head and kiss the smooth, tender flesh of her neck. "Don't be long. It's been a long day and I'm looking forward to hearing your feminine cries of pleasure."

The pupils of her purple eyes dilate as a sultry smile blooms. "Don't start without me."

"No promises." I watch the graceful sway of her silver hair as it brushes over her perfect ass.

I could take in that view all day long.

Alone with the anticipation of what comes next, I study the tray Jaxx sent us up with. It looks innocuous enough. A pitcher of fruity delight with five glasses to keep the buzz going, a tray of nibbles to keep up our strength, and a treasure chest about the size of a shoebox labeled, 'an evening of fun'.

"Have you looked inside?" Dune asks, eyeing up the treasure chest as he and Shadow come in for the night.

"I haven't. I figure it'll be more fun if we're all shocked together."

"Shocked? Do you think it'll be inappropriate?"

I bark a laugh. "It definitely will. Jaxx doesn't have boundary lines like most people."

Dune unbuckles his boots and leaves them beside the door. "My kind of guy."

Moonshade bounds over and stands on her back legs to reach up and see me. I pick her up and look deep into her eyes. "Any chance I can entice you into a few hours of sex, counselor?"

Shadow takes three tentative steps forward, touches the back of the couch, and uses the edge of the furniture to walk around it and sit down beside me. "Is there anyone who says no to that?"

"I suppose it's possible."

"Those people might need counseling."

"True. Either that or they don't have the kind of partners we do."

"That's also possible."

He leans toward me, and I meet his kiss.

Lips touch lips and I let out a soft sigh. The tension of the past two days—of Shadow's seizure, Dune's injuries, and tonight's battle—was pushed to the background, but with Shadow's lips on mine, I'm finally able to let it go.

Each of my mates has a different kiss: Honor's is passionate and demanding, Tundra's is tentative and hot, Dune's is playful and daring, and Shadow's is searing and emotional.

The room spins in a warm, sexy haze, as his tongue teases mine. The tang of ale and the sweet body of bourbon mix in our mouths. His hand slides across my ribs and the evening is off to a good start.

My shirt was already undone, so he has full access to my chest.

Damn, what is it that drives my hunger for him?

I can't get enough.

And it's not just him. I'm just as horny for Honor and

Tundra. Dune and I have come a long way and even he sparks heat deep inside me.

"Hey, are you two starting without us?" Honor asks, chuckling.

Shadow and I ease apart but I don't let him go far. "Nope. Just getting warmed up. We were just discussing Jaxx's sexy game night and the probability that it will be horribly inappropriate."

Honor laughs. "My favorite kind of sex games."

"Exactly what *I* said." Dune sits down and reaches for the finger foods. We've got small pastries, sliced meats, warm cheeses, and pita chips to spread it on. "So, is there an advantage to being dressed or undressed in this game? What do our starting positions look like?"

I shrug. "He didn't say. I suppose we can make that call on our own."

Honor grins. "Then down to boxers and panties we go. We don't want to get started until Tundra gets back. I'm sure some of the fun will be undressing one another."

"I love this game already," Dune says.

The four of us strip down to our last layer and get started on the pitcher of Jaxx's fruity concoction.

When I take my first few swallows, I whistle between my teeth. "Wow. That has one hell of a kick."

Honor swirls the deep, burgundy liquid in the bottom of her tumbler and watches it dance up the side of the crystal. "Creed and I went to the Haze distillery with our father when we were kids. The Mix Master told us the secret to its fruity sweetness is in the ripeness of the jorgan berry. It has to be picked just before it's ripe so that by the time it's sorted, cleaned, and crushed, it's perfect."

I chuckle, looking at the liquid in my tumbler. "I'm not sure there are any actual fruits in this. Other than wine and some daquiris, our booze doesn't come from real fruit."

"It's still tasty, though," Dune says.

We're on our second top-ups when Tundra comes in, studies us all in our skivvies, and arches a brow. "Did I miss the starting bell?"

I pour him a glass and stand to offer it to him. "Not yet, but we were about to drag you up here if you didn't get back soon. Lock the door for the night, Iceman. It's time to get this party started."

Honor claps her hands. "Take off your clothes, T. Oh, and make sure to give us our bubble of privacy, magic man. I don't intend to be a lady tonight."

That little declaration zings straight to my groin. As the tingle of things waking up takes hold, I do as she asks and cast us a veil of privacy.

Once that's done, I address the treasure chest. "All right, so, in the spirit of sexy shenanigans, let's see what Jaxx has in store for us, shall we?"

The lid of the box opens on a hinge, so I can see what's inside, but the others can't yet. There's a note for one player to be the game master. I grab the paper, let the box fall closed, and read the instructions. "Okay, I think I've got this. Who wants to go first?"

"Definitely me." Dune sets his drink onto the table and rubs his palms together. "What do I do?"

I lift the lid of the box so I can see but they can't. With a quick selection, I take out the action cards and the colored spinner. "The first round goes until everyone is naked. Do you want to give or receive for your turn?"

He licks his lips and swallows. "Give."

Huh, I would've guessed Dune was all about receiving. I like that he's still surprising me. "All right, spin the spinner to choose your partner for your turn."

I set the spinner wheel on the table and slide it across to our desert mate. He flicks his finger and sets it spinning.

When the arrow slows to a stop, it's on the wedge marked Shadow.

Dune waggles his brows. "Looks like we're up, counselor."

Of all of us, Shadow and Dune have had the least direct contact, so this is good. At first, Dune was opposed to having Shadow in our mating group, but I'm happy to say he's gotten past that now.

"All right, I'm supposed to lay out five rows of five cards face down. You're going to randomly pick three cards, read them, and decide which of the tasks you want to do with Shadow."

Dune laughs and cracks his knuckles. "Done."

"You read the other two aloud and set them back down in the array as your discards. The rest of us need to remember what cards are where so that when it's our turn if there's something we want to do or have done to us, we know where that card is. Got it?"

"Got it." Honor is grinning as she drops onto her knees on the floor to get closer to the table. "It's an erotic version of a memory game."

"Right you are, babe." I shuffle the cards and then set them out, face down on the table. "All right, Dune, pick your three."

Dune studies the backs of the cards and chooses the three he wants to read. He reads them to himself first, laughs, and then sets his choice face down. "The two I'm not choosing but sound awesome are: Make your partner a work of art with edible body paint or challenge your partner to a naked pillow fight."

"I like both of those," Tundra says, watching where Dune puts them back.

I laugh at his enthusiasm. "Trust me, Tundra, Jaxx made this game. I bet they're all good."

"Okay, so what did you pick?" Honor asks.

Dune picks up his card. "Insert a vibrating toy into your partner."

I laugh at the look Shadow gives us before he downs the rest of his drink. "Am I to assume the position somewhere?"

I open the treasure chest and select two of the male anal toys I have to offer. "With cock ring attachment or without, Dune?"

He laughs. "Is that even a serious question? Definitely with."

I open the sealed packaging, hand him the silky toy, and add in a bottle of lube. "Do your thing."

Tundra shifts out of the way and gives Dune and Shadow space. Honor is still on the floor and smiles at me. "Are there rules about joining the fun?"

I glance back at the rules and shake my head. "Nope. It says everything is fair play as long as you don't impede the task at hand." Honor is on her third drink and feeling it. Her cheeks are flushed and when she gets like this, she gets handsy and horny.

"I wouldn't dream of impeding anything." Rising to her feet, she takes Shadow's hand and bites her bottom lip. "Come with me, boys, I'm going to help."

I sit back, chuckling to myself as Honor leads the two of them around to the back of the couch. "Shadow, I'd like to strip you naked and put the ring around your cock, then I'm going to get on my knees and suck on you while you bend over for Dune. Sound good?"

Shadow swallows. "Sounds perfect."

Tundra pulls out his tablet, calls up something on the screen and then music starts playing. It's not like anything you'd hear in the Human Realm. It's a crossover between blues and something with a Celtic rhythm to it.

It's good though, and low enough that it's not distracting.

When he's done playing Mr. DJ, Tundra sits on the arm of the couch next to me. It's erotic as hell for the two of us to watch Honor slide her fingers into the waistband of Shadow's boxers and then sink to the floor and out of our vision.

Not that we don't know exactly what she's doing.

Shadow's body shudders and he leans forward, resting his arms on the back of the couch.

"Our princess does have a hot and greedy mouth, doesn't she, Counsellor?" Dune says standing behind him watching with a grin.

"No complaints here," Shadow chokes.

"Fuck, things are getting too confining," I say, standing to pull off my own boxers.

"Agreed." Tundra rids himself of his own.

The two of us, naked and next to one another makes it so much harder not to start something.

"How's it going over there, you three?"

"Just about to turn on the vibrator," Dune says, grinning.

Shadow's eyes roll back and then his hips start a slow grind forward.

"You guys are coloring outside the lines here," I say, gripping my cock to give it a couple of strokes. "Honor, he's not supposed to be fucking your mouth. This is Dune's turn."

The moist *pop* of her releasing his cock makes my erection bob. "Sorry, I was just getting things started. My turn next."

She rounds the couch and kneels at the table. With a flick of her finger, she sends the spinner flying around in circles to determine her partner. "Tundra." Grabbing two cards, she reads them and makes a snap decision. "I want to receive. I'm not choosing play naked tic-tac-toe with our bodies as a game board and I *am* picking, Have sex outdoors."

She gets up and practically runs for the balcony, wriggling her ass as she shoves her panties down her thighs and unbuckles her bra.

Tundra looks at me and I laugh. "You better catch up, Iceman. It seems our girl is in a hurry to have your cock inside her."

"Yes, I am," she calls out to us, "and I won't apologize for it."

"No apologies ever, babe." I grab the spinner and flick the arrow around. "I got you, Honor."

"Yay! What are you going to do to me?"

I pick two cards, make my choice, and show it to Dune first, and then I hold it in front of Moonshade.

Shadow's smile is so incredibly sinful my cock weeps in anticipation. "Playfully paddle, or feather tickle your partner. I like it."

Me too.

I flip the lid of the box open and yep, tools of the trade are here. Damn. This is going to get good.

CHAPTER NINETEEN

Honor

$\mathcal{T}$he balcony off our guest suite extends far enough that we have space to spread out but also has slatted wooden walls at both sides that hang thick with greenery to give us privacy. It's lovely, actually.

I make a mental note to have something similar built on our suite back home.

After all, with two Elbirfae who fly in and out, an elf who feels most at home in nature, and me, a girl who needs to do a lot more communing with nature than I currently do, a private balcony makes sense.

Or at least, that will be what I tell people.

Having orgasms in the moonlight with a cool breeze chilling my heated skin will be the real reason.

With my back pressed against the wall, Tundra lifts me in slow and steady thrusts, filling me and then retreating, building my need, giving me everything, and at the same time, making me ache for more.

"Tundra, you feel too good inside me," I gasp, my head falling to the side as he drops his mouth to my neck.

He drags his tongue along the line of my throat, burning a singeing trail of seduction. Then, as he continues to lave my neck, the breeze catches the moisture on my skin, and I'm covered in the most delicious goosebumps.

The strength of the man is incredible.

He has a hold on my thighs and I swear he could keep pounding inside me for hours without ever feeling the strain of keeping me in the air.

"I chose my card, Princess," Lukas says, joining us. "I'm to either playful paddle or feather tickle you."

The graveled edge to Lukas's voice tells me how turned on he is. I'm not sure if it's the prospect of light BDSM or watching Tundra grind into me...

Honestly, I don't care.

A light gust of wind hits and I shiver.

"Look at those nipples," Lukas says. "Tundra, come lay her down on the patio table. You can keep fucking her while I play my card."

"Just don't make him pull out. I never want him to leave."

Lukas laughs. "That might make his warrior life more difficult, but that's fine. You heard the lady, T. Don't ever leave the sweet heat of her pussy."

"If you insist." Tundra adjusts his hold on me and moves us over to the seating area by the living wall. Tilting me back, he rests my butt on the table, lays me back, and then hooks his arms under my legs.

Knowing the table is made out of wood and tiles, I expect it to be cold. It's not. There's a thick blanket draped over the entire surface. "Sweet mercies, is this blanket heated?"

Lukas waggles his brows at me. "We don't want you to catch a chill, now do we, Princess?"

I relax into the warmth of the blanket and watch the delicious flex and release of Tundra's abs as he fucks me. He has the body of a sculpted god.

A masterpiece.

"Do you like what you see, Princess?" he asks, his voice husky.

"Very much," I say, my release building in the rippling waves starting to take hold within. "Even sexier though is that you belong to me. You are mine."

"I do and I am."

He pushes inside me and stills, pressing his palm over my bare belly. "Sometimes I'm so far inside you I swear I must be pushing here."

It feels like it. Tundra is a big boy. When he's inside me, the stretch of my body to accept him is almost too much.

Almost...but *not* too much.

Never too much.

Lukas moves in with a gleam in his eyes and a suede flogger in his hand. He dangles the tendrils of brushed leather over my breastbone and starts a circuit around my breasts.

"Ooo, that feels nice."

He finishes the gentle sweep of suede over my skin and then lifts his hand and gives a snap of his wrist. The tendrils of leather hit first one nipple and then the other. The stark contrast between soft and sharp makes my heart pump harder.

"Look at how hard those nipples are peaked," Lukas says, teasing.

"Don't mind if we do." Dune leads Shadow out by his cock and then the gang is all here. The black ring banding his shaft is attached to the vibrator and is keeping the toy in place.

He's rock solid.

"That's one beautiful sight," Dune says.

"Yes, it is," I say, staring at Shadow.

Lukas chuckles, makes another circuit with the flogger, and

once again ends with a snap to each of my nipples. "I think he was talking about *you*, babe."

Was he? I'm too far gone to pay attention.

Lukas trails the soft strands of the flogger over my breasts, and I groan. My body is strung tight under the seductive play, my orgasm closing in fast.

"Do you want more, Princess?" Lukas asks.

"Yes, please."

"Such a well-mannered girl. And here you said you weren't going to be a lady tonight." He lowers the flogger and does another circuit around the fleshy mounds of my breasts before snapping his wrist and sending zings of sensation through me. "What have you got there, Shadow?"

Shadow smiles and holds up four different colored tubes. "I picked edible body paint. Being blind might be a bit of a challenge when painting Honor. I'm going to have to depend on my sense of touch and the help of you guys."

Lukas grins. "We're here for you, my man. Whatever you need."

"He needs to do something with that erection of his," I say, sucking in a deep breath. "That's a beautiful thing, Shadow."

"Thank you. This vibrator is quite wonderful. I think I may need to claim it to take home."

Lukas takes that moment to whip my nipples and I hiss and arch my back. "Dirty pool, magic man. I was distracted by Shadow's cock."

Damn. As my words ring in my ears, it cranks me up even more. Four incredibly sexy men...all naked...all sporting beautiful hard-ons.

"Shadow, you play with me, and I'll play with you. Deal?" I don't wait for his response. I reach to the edge of the table and wrap my fingers around his cock.

His body shudders, bending over the table while he catches

his breath. I give him a moment to settle and then begin a slow and gentle rhythm.

"I'm lopsided. I want another cock in this hand." I flex my fingers of my free hand and a moment later Dune is there for me to hold onto. "Good man. That's much better."

Closing my eyes, I revel in the slow and sensual fuck of Tundra while I toss Dune and Shadow root to tip. It's incredible...except there's one man left out.

"Lukas, climb onto the table and straddle my head. I want to suck on you."

The deep, throaty chuckle of his amusement hits me right where Tundra is pumping. "I think you've got your hands full already, Princess."

"I know I do, but not my mouth. Come on now, do as I say. I command you to fuck my mouth so I can have all four of your cocks at one time."

Lukas swallows and looks at me. "Well, when you put it like that...who am I to ignore the command of the realm princess?"

It doesn't take him long to climb onto the table. When he's on his hands and knees, he positions himself so I can suck him into my mouth.

The moment the salty warmth of his pre-cum hits my tongue, I'm lost to the pleasures of all four of my mates at once.

The tension building in my womb tightens and I embrace this. The stretching glide and slide of Tundra filling me, the gentle pump of Lukas's hips as I suck him off, and the soft flesh gliding over steel shafts in each of my hands.

This.

This is my life.

They are my life.

Tundra

Ecstasy. Of all the moments in my life, this one stands out as the most transcendent. Being buried in my bonded female while feeling the tremors of her pending release gripping me. Smelling the arousal of not only her but of all of us. Hearing the throaty moans as all five of us find pleasure in one another.

It's ecstasy.

It's also too much.

If I revel in the glory of it too much longer, I'm going to lose focus and finish. Orgasms are a tricky thing. You feel so good and look forward to that moment so much but the last thing you want is for the feeling to end.

Slow and steady might win the race but it deprives both lovers of that heightened sensation that only comes when the blood is pumping, and our hearts are threatening to pound out of our chest.

That's what this moment calls for.

Picking up the pace of my thrusts, I secure my hold on Honor's legs and raise the bar.

Harder and faster, I bring us together, the moist *slap, slap, slap* of flesh filling the air.

Ecstasy. My muscles are tired from use but there's no way I'm not going to finish strong. I hammer inside her, using my hold on her legs to pull her into my thrusts.

Honor's throaty groan escapes from around Lukas's cock and tells me how hungry she is for more.

My breath quickens and my wings flare out behind me. Using the leverage of my feathered appendages, I'm able to bolster my strength.

My release builds in my balls, the tingle of cum pushing hard against the base of my cock. I close my eyes to make sure Honor goes off first. The visual stimulation of my mates having sex is too hot...too much.

And while Honor is close...I might be closer.

The inner quakes of her muscles have grown greedy, gripping me as I glide in and out of her heated depths. She's so wet. And tight. And hot...

Sweat slicks my skin and the kiss of the outdoors cools me off.

"Are you good with me coming like this?" Lukas gasps, his hips rocking into her mouth. "If you aren't, now is the time to let me know."

Honor makes no move to release him.

"Oh, teeth," Lukas hisses. "Okay, I'm not going anywhere."

I try not to chuckle but it's difficult. Honor is an aggressive lover and yes, when she gets wound up, she is a bit of a biter.

Lukas is the first to orgasm. His hips thrust forward and the throaty grunt of his release spilling out of him sets off a chain reaction.

Honor groans as her hips start to buck. The pleasures overtaking her bombard and her body grips and releases, milking me.

That's my cue to let loose. Without the fear of going off too soon, my thrusts grow wild and carnal.

Sweet mercy I feel incredible inside her.

The scrape of the table legs against the balcony floor becomes a steady beat of my thrusts. There's a railing keeping us from going over the edge, so I don't let the prospect of moving furniture slow me down.

My head is spinning, the burning need to mark her rising to detonation within.

I come in a surge of emotion, my release a cresting wave of pleasure exploding out of me with a primal rightness. I'm racked with waves of release...lose all sense of my surroundings.

There is just me inside my female, with the incredible view of Dune and Shadow gripping the edge of the patio table as they spill across Honor's gripping and pumping hands.

Dune looks like he might pass out and Shadow looks...he looks a little sad, actually.

No one else seems to notice Shadow's shift in mood. Everyone is lost in their moments of completion, but it hurts my heart.

He hasn't found his true happiness with us yet. Is it his condition? Is it the fact that he's blind and can't see what's going on with us?

Without speaking to him, there's no way to know.

This isn't the time.

If he wanted to share his heartaches, he wouldn't work so hard to hide them from the rest of us. I file that away for the moment and make a mental note to speak to him privately the first moment we're alone with one another.

"Well, that was fun," Lukas says, dismounting the table and waggling his brows. "Except Shadow didn't get to paint Honor."

"Who says the night is over?" Honor says, raising her arms and stretching so that her body undulates in the light like a seductive goddess. "By all means, Counselor. Open your paints and take your turn. Nothing should stand in the way of art."

"I vote we clean up, grab a bite to eat, and plan for round two?" Dune waits for everyone to weigh in and then heads inside. A moment later, he returns with a warm cloth and a towel. "Might as well clean up before we make our next mess."

He tosses me the warm cloth and I wipe Honor's arms where Dune and Shadow left their marks and then move to where I had my fun. "That was wonderful."

"It was," Dune says. "Brant is always saying Jaxx has a creative flare they enjoy."

Honor chuckles. "Well, if this game is any indication of what they get up to on a regular basis, I'd say Brant's right."

Lukas rolls his eyes. "Oh, this is definitely what they're like on a regular basis. I'm just thankful I'm not the one listening to them all orgasm in the next room anymore. A guy can only toss off in the shower so many times before it gets weird."

"I bet," Honor laughs. When I'm finished cleaning Honor, she hops off the table and gestures inside to where Dune and Lukas have descended on our snack tray and our pitcher of drinks. "Are you boys coming inside for a snack?"

"In a second," I say, heading over to Shadow. "You go ahead."

When Honor is inside and they are engaged in conversation, I take a moment to tend to Shadow. In a soft voice, I lean in and speak privately to him. "Are you well? I noticed you looked sad a moment ago."

He tenses and glances toward where the others are talking. "Did they see?"

"No. It was just me who noticed. I won't say anything. I just wanted to check in with you."

Shadow swallows and steps back, leaning against the edge of the table. "I appreciate that. It's fine. I'm fine. It's just been a tough time."

"Absolutely. So, if you *weren't* fine, you could tell me, and I wouldn't judge. I'm your mate and I'm here for you."

He takes the towel from me and runs it over his abs and groin. "All right, if I'm being truthful, I'm not doing well. The problem is, I don't know how to fix it or if it can be fixed at all."

"And when you say *it*, what are you referring to?"

He lifts a shoulder. "Everything and nothing. I'm thankful for all of you and the life we're building but I'm not the man I want to be in this quint."

"That could be temporary."

"It could be. Or, maybe in six months or a year, we'll be in a moment like this, and instead of seeing my lovers I'll still be stuck watching Moonshade licking herself."

Oh no. "Is that what you were seeing just now?"

He exhales a heavy breath and his shoulders slump. "I'm not trying to sound ungrateful, I'm truly not, but there are no good answers for me right now. I want to be a man of purpose and not the broken piece of the puzzle. "

I pull him into my arms and wrap my wings around us both. "I promise we don't think of you that way. And whatever it takes, we're going to find a way to handle your transition and keep you from getting worse."

"I truly believe Calli's tears are the answer, but Lukas is blocking me. He wants to study the possible outcomes and research the contraindications. I just want to give it a try. It's my body. I should be the one to make that decision."

And now I understand why Shadow hasn't said anything. His closest confidants are Lukas and Honor and they, for sure, won't even entertain the idea of moving too quickly on this and endangering him.

"I'll talk to them," I say, easing back from our embrace. "I'll think of a way to make them see your need for resolution and I'll talk to them."

Shadow grips my jaw with both hands, rises on his toes, and brushes his lips over mine. The kiss is reverent and sweet and my heart breaks a little more. "Thank you, Tundra. You don't know how much this means to me."

CHAPTER TWENTY

*L*ukas

The morning after the night before, the five of us are flying high on pheromones and the adrenaline of a night of orgasms. It's crazy what a little playtime can do. Or in our case...a lot of playtime.

"What's the plan for today?" Dune flips a mug from the tray beside the coffee maker and proceeds to fill up at the fueling station. "Do we have any idea how we're going to find Ruic Breard?"

I finish scrolling through the morning reports on my laptop and close things up for breakfast. "I do. Hawk and I were chatting about that last night. As far as we know, Ruic Breard is the only goblin in this realm and we're fairly certain he's still here because we locked down the gatehouse to anyone except us."

Honor and Tundra come in together and head straight for the covered platters of quiche and hashbrowns. "Oh, my goodness, this smells so good."

Jaxx winks, standing to surrender his place at the table. "And it does Mama's heart good to cook for a full house."

"Well, she's amazing," Honor says.

"Absolutely," Calli says. "I'd be lost without her. The only reason I can handle a newborn and four mates and being Fae Prima is because of Jaxx's parents."

Jaxx shakes his head. "They're not just my parents anymore. When we mated and took on this life together, they became all of our parents."

"I'm honored to accept," Calli says.

Honor and Tundra sit down opposite me with filled plates.

"One thing you can't miss about Elbirfae is that you eat twice as much as the rest of us," I say, astounded at the mountain of food on Tundra's plate.

"It takes a lot to fuel these perfect bodies," Dune says, setting his mug down at his place before turning back to stack his own plate.

"But you're right, Princess. This smells amazing."

"And tastes even better." Honor groans as she chews, closing her eyes as she swallows. "Where's Shadow? Did he take Moonshade outside before he ate?"

I ease my mug back from my lips and frown. "He hasn't come in. I thought he was upstairs with you."

Honor shakes her head and glances around the massive eat-in kitchen. "No. He told us he wanted to come down to get his coffee and chat with you about something."

All of a sudden, my spidey senses are tingling. Standing, I round the table and start the hunt. Dune, Tundra, and Honor are right behind me. When your mate has an ailment that causes him to seize and lose consciousness, you worry when he's suddenly unaccounted for.

"Maybe he took Moonshade out for a quick pee before breakfast," Honor says, heading for the front door.

"Moonshade!" I let off a whistle and call our baby wolf. The excited yips that come back to me aren't coming from outside, they're coming from the private library in the front of the house.

The door is closed and now that we're calling her, our little wolf is scratching at the back of the door.

My quick stride ramps up to a panicked jog. "Shadow? Are you all right?"

I twist the knob and rush through the door, bumping Moonshade and sweeping her along in the swing of things. "Sorry, sweet girl. Where is he?"

Glancing around the space, I jog past the first couple of shelves and see Shadow sitting in the chair facing the window. "Shadow? Are you all right?"

The fact that he's not answering me is tripping every panic button I've got. I'm at his side and facing him two racing heartbeats later.

All the blood rushes from my head when I see him. He's unconscious and the usual warm bronze of his skin is sallow and pale. "Hey, there, Counselor. Are you with us?" I press my fingers against his neck and my panic increases. "Someone get Doc."

Honor shakes his head. "They took Keyla back to Dornte last night."

"Then Jaxx." I straighten and shout toward the door. "Jaxx! We need you in the library!"

"Tundra, help me lay him down on the area rug. Dune, move the chair out of the way."

The three of us scramble to get him laid out and by the time he's on his back, Jaxx is rushing in with a medical bag. "Was he unconscious when you found him?"

"Yes."

"He wasn't seizing or having an episode?"

"No."

Jaxx uses his thumbs to open Shadow's eyes. He shines the pencil light in them and frowns. "Huh."

"What?" I ask, shifting around Jaxx's shoulder so I can see. "What's huh?"

He abandons his study of Shadow's eyes and presses his fingers into the pulse on his wrist. "I'm not sure how to gauge his eyes like this. The oracle thing is not in my wheelhouse."

"I've been training with Demarco," Honor says, shifting to sit on her knees at Shadow's head. "Damn it, I wish Creed was here to help."

Honor sandwiches Shadow's temples with both her palms. Bending over his head, she closes her eyes. Our princess doesn't talk much about her Mind Guardian magic, mostly because she doesn't consider it magic. To her, it's just a genetic ability like her being able to release her wings and fly.

Which, I explained to her was also magical.

The thumping of running feet brings Kotah, and Calli into the mix.

"What can I do?" Kotah asks.

I run my fingers through my hair, the lump in my throat making it hard to swallow. "I don't know. We don't know what's wrong with him."

"I have a guess," Calli says, reaching over to the shelf beside the chair Shadow was in. She lifts up one of the little glass vials we store Calli's tears in. "I'm guessing he downed a vial of my tears."

I close my eyes, fighting the urge to curse him out. "I told him we'd have to talk to Demarco…that we needed to research the damage caused by the oracle fracturing."

Jaxx sits back and frowns. "I'd say he wasn't on board with that plan."

"He wasn't," Tundra says. "He confessed that to me last night and I assured him I would speak to you, and we'd work it out."

"And now what?" I gesture to him lying unconscious on the floor. "How do we work *this* out?"

"Easy," Hawk says, gripping my shoulder. "None of this is Tundra's fault."

I hear the suggestive tone in Hawk's voice and take the hint.

Meeting Tundra's gaze, I rein in my panic. "No, of course, it isn't. I'm just scared. I'm sorry. None of this is on you."

"Let's keep in mind, my tears have never harmed anyone," Calli says.

I sigh. "There's a lot going on with Shadow's oracle genes sparking to life we don't understand. Even something as restorative as your tears could work differently on him. They could make things worse."

"Or they could make things better."

Hawk sighs and waves his hand in the air to cut off the conversation. "How about we don't borrow trouble where there might not be any to find?"

I want to tell him to fuck his platitudes, but I bite my tongue. "We don't know if Shadow's condition will count as an injury, if he's finished evolving, or if the tears will even affect his genes activating."

Hawk meets my gaze and offers me a sympathetic smile. "I guess we're going to find out."

~

Tundra

"How is he doing?" Calli asks as the four of us exit our guest room and meet her, Kotah, Brant, and Hawk in the hall.

Honor hugs her best friend and then the two of them ease apart. "We have no idea. From the look of things, Jaxx thinks he's resting comfortably, but there's no way to know."

Calli brushes a piece of Honor's hair back. "Then you and your mates should leave him with us and go find your bad guy. The sooner Ruic Breard is apprehended and removed from the playing board, the sooner you can take Shadow home and have Demarco and Doc look at him."

"I can't leave him," she says.

"No, you can't," Lukas agrees. "You're the only one who can minimalize the fracturing. You should stay here. Dune, Tundra, and I will track down Breard and put an end to this."

Honor looks torn, but Lukas is right. She's the only one here who can actively ease the progression of Shadow's symptoms if something happens.

"Why don't we start with tracking Breard down and then we'll check-in and see if there's any change," I suggest. "That way, you won't necessarily be missing the takedown and you're here with Jaxx if Shadow takes a turn for the worse."

"Or he could take a turn for the better," Dune says, holding up his finger. "Like Calli said, her tears have only ever healed people. I, for one, am living proof that little vial of fluid can do magical things."

I meet Lukas's and Honor's gaze. "We need to assume that's the case until something proves us wrong. If we don't, we won't be able to function. Dornte needs its Guardians of the Crown to end this. Agreed?"

"Agreed." Lukas hugs Honor and turns to Jaxx. "If anything happens…"

Jaxx nods and pats Lukas's arm. "We'll let you know. Now, go on. Catch yourself a goblin."

Honor, Calli, and Jaxx head back into the suite while Hawk leads the way and the rest of us go downstairs.

"So," Lukas says, once we're in the security office. "The way I see it, we need to find Breard. We need to nullify his Law of Leadership agreement. And we need to ensure no one comes back at Kotah for what happened with the Fae Council?"

Kotah lifts his shoulders. "Whatever happens next, I don't regret it. But it makes sense that I'm the one who goes to the Bastion to check on the filed petition. And yes, I should double-check that my throne is still mine to rule."

Brant chuckles. "I'm fairly certain your point was made. Anyone still alive on the Fae Council is either smart enough or loyal enough to want last night's little misunderstanding to go away."

Kotah removes his choker and slides it into his pocket. "Still, it can't hurt to make sure."

"No, it can't," Hawk says. "Brant, you're with Kotah. Straight there and straight back. We'll do our thing here and we'll meet up as soon as we can."

"Done deal," Brant says heading toward the hallway. "We'll be back."

When the two of them leave, Lukas looks at Hawk. "So, I've been thinking about how to track down Breard and I'm wondering if maybe the portal composite file can help us. If we can modify the search parameters to specifically home in on his species, we should be able to find him."

"What's a portal composite file?" Dune asks.

Hawk takes that one and pulls out his fancy, silver, cigarette holder. "When we pass through the portal gate, the entire makeup of our body is scanned and saved in a backup file system."

"Why?" Tundra asks.

"Originally to ensure that no matter the race or species of fae traveling through the portal gate, the system didn't interfere with their natural biology. In the early days of portal systems in this realm, some species ended up on the opposite end of their transport with unwanted side-effects."

Dune's brow pinches. "That doesn't instill my confidence in your portal system."

Hawk chuckles. "As I said, this was in the *early* days of portal systems. Our design architects worked out those bugs long ago, but it's policy to create composite files for travelers regardless."

Lukas accepts a cigarette, lights up, and draws a deep pull. When he exhales, he's noticeably more relaxed. "So, my idea is to take the composite file for Enrich Glades, a.k.a. Ruic Breard, and modify our FCO satellite tracking to focus on his goblin genes."

I follow his line of thinking. In theory, it's a solid strategy. "And because goblins have never lived in the Human Realm, he should be the only one here who carries that gene."

Lukas nods and offers me his smoke. "Exactly. The FCO tracking systems have, on occasion, piggybacked onto the human satellite systems. I'm thinking we can get in, search, pinpoint our bad guy, and scoop him up before he even knows we're coming."

Dune reaches for the cigarette next and smiles as the effects take hold. "Oh, this is nice."

"You're welcome," Hawk says, grinning. "Now, all we have to do is make it happen and then initiate the goblin takedown."

Dune passes the hand-rolled back to Lukas and smiles. "And, just to be clear, what is our objective when taking him down? Do we want to arrest him? Make him suffer? Or do we finally get to end this?"

Lukas pegs us both with a serious look. "Honor and Creed spoke last night and it's decided. The first person to get an opportunity takes him down. No questions. No hesitation."

I stretch my wings out eager to get to the takedown part of the day. "Not a problem. You boys track him, and Dune and I will end this rebellion once and for all."

CHAPTER TWENTY-ONE

Lukas

*I*t takes Hawk and me just over an hour to collect the data we need from the portal filters, isolate them, recalibrate them to only focus on the goblin gene, and then filter them through the FCO manhunt program.

Once everything is loaded and ready to go, I straighten. "Now we wait."

"How long will it take?" Tundra asks.

"That depends on what rock Breard crawled under when he teleported away from the Bastion. The farther from here and the more remote the location, the longer it'll take for the system to track him."

"Assuming we're right and the recalibrations are actually tracking down the goblin genes," Hawk says.

I frown at him. "We're right. Trust me, I went over the calculations four times. If he's in this realm, we'll get him."

Dune nods. "If we're waiting, can we set a timer on things here and check in with Honor and Jaxx?"

It does my heart good to see the growing concern in Dune's

behavior. He truly is embracing us as his mates. "Yeah, let's do that and get a bite to eat too. We don't know when we'll get the notification or how long we'll be gone. You boys need to fuel those bodies, and I need to make sure you're well topped up for what comes next."

"Damn straight," Dune says, heading for the door. "I'll check on the lunch plans and then meet you upstairs. Maggie mentioned something about down-home southern cooking. I'm not sure what that means but, by Jaxx's reaction, it sounded good."

While Dune and Tundra go to the kitchen, I jog up the stairs two at a time and make my way to our guest suite. It was incredibly thoughtful of Hawk, Calli, and the quint to plan a suite for not only us but for Creed and Keyla's group too.

Somehow, I went from being an only child who spent most of my life on the outside looking in, to this crazy group of found family. Fourteen of us mated and joined as in-laws.

Seventeen when I add Jaxx's parents and Skye.

Opening the door, I let myself in. Honor meets me with a hug, and I take the moment to reset. My princess is tall and athletic, but as strong a female as she is, there are still plenty of soft, curvy parts to cushion against my hard plains.

"Hey, magic man. How goes the goblin hunt?" Her breath is warm on my neck, her voice a soft caress in my whirring mind.

"So far, so good. I think we've calibrated the equipment to do the searching for us. If I've done my job right, Hawk's million-dollar systems are closing in on Ruic Breard as we speak."

"Then I have no doubt that's what will happen. Thank the fae universe for you."

I chuckle. "The whole universe, eh? That's quite a compliment."

"You deserve it."

We stay like that, linked in a warm embrace until I realize it's too intimate for the company sharing the room with us.

"Sorry, Jaxx." I step back from my princess and turn to him. "How is our patient doing?"

He shrugs. "The same? Better maybe? Since there are no actual signs of distress, it's hard to say if things are getting better."

"Are they getting worse?"

"No. I don't think so. Again, to me, it seems like he's sleeping as peacefully as he did after the accident."

I wander to the bed and sit on the edge of the mattress. Jaxx isn't wrong when he says it seems like Shadow's sleeping. With his purple hair soft against the pillows and his eyes closed, he looks as peaceful as he has since this all began.

More peaceful even.

I think about what Jaxx said about the accident. He hit his head against the window of the truck when I swerved to avoid the incoming missile. Those days when Shadow lay in that coma my guts were twisted in knots.

That was when I realized my affections for him had grown in the weeks we tended to Honor's needs.

That was also when Doc first discovered Shadow was experiencing a metamorphosis of sorts.

Is that what's happening now? Is this another level of change occurring?

Maybe this has nothing to do with Calli's tears or his body's reaction to them. Maybe this is phase two of his transitioning. What could that even mean?

I think about the empty vial sitting next to him in that window seat and discount the idea.

No. It's too coincidental. Whatever is happening now is definitely connected to him swallowing that vial of tears.

"Damn it, Shadow. Why couldn't you just be patient and believe in me?"

A strong hand grips my shoulder and then Tundra bends to

kiss my temple. "He believes in you. That's not what this was about."

"No? Then what? Why would he risk harming himself just to rush for a cure?"

"He told me he's not the man he wants to be in this quint. He feels broken, like he has no purpose, like he doesn't offer anything to the four of us. It's worse when we're together like we were last night."

The gasp of air that escapes my lungs leaves me breathless. As I stare at him, the moisture in my eyes blurs my vision. "How could he feel like that? He's our guiding logic, our tether to home and heart."

"He is, but prior to his genes taking over his life, he was an independent professional. As a man, you must understand what a blow it is to have that taken away. He lost his patients, his purpose, his sight, and his understanding of who he is."

"He is our mate. That's who he is." My tears run in warm runnels down my cheeks, and I don't even try to stop them or fake that I'm okay.

I'm not.

Honor crawls onto the other side of the bed and reaches over to hold my hand. "Why don't you lay with us for a few minutes before you go again. Maybe it'll make you feel better."

I draw a deep breath and scrub my palms over my cheeks. "No. If I stay, I'm going to give in to my heartache and I can't afford that right now. Later, once Breard is out of the way, I'll fall apart, but not now."

I lean toward the center of the mattress and kiss Honor before standing and pulling myself together. "Tundra? Are you coming down to grab a bite to eat before we go, or do you want to stay a little longer?"

Tundra laces his fingers with mine and squeezes. "I'm with you. We'll get things done and then get back where we belong."

I nod. "Yeah, let's getter done."

～

Dune

Lunch is a solemn affair. We eat for the sustenance of it, but our minds and hearts are upstairs with our mate. Wow, being in a committed relationship can really weigh on your emotions.

It's weird.

If I knew upfront that being mated would mean I'd be worried and twisted up every time one of them suffered, I don't know that I would've been up for it.

Now that I have them and they're mine, I can't imagine anything else.

What is life about if not to share it with people who love you?

"How is Shadow?" Skye asks, sitting at the table with Tundra and me.

"He's resting," Tundra says.

"Do you know what's happening with him yet?" Yarko asks.

"No. Not yet. Still, Jaxx is hopeful he's in a healing sleep. Once we take care of our business tracking down Ruic Breard, we'll get him home. I'm sure he'll wake up wondering why all of us look so worried."

Skye brightens at the idea. "I bet that's true. Hey, speaking of going home, Yarko and I were talking. Would it be okay if he stays with us for a bit and maybe learns about being an Amberloq Warrior? He has no real family, like us, and I thought..."

The hopeful light in Yarko's eyes is too funny. Were we all so transparently eager to be heroes at that age? Was I that desperate?

Yeah. Maybe even more so.

Tundra dips his chin and extends his hand. "Of course. You're more than welcome to come. You'll have to sit through an uncomfortable conversation about what I'll do to you if you overstep with Skye or any of the other females, but you can come."

"You're hilarious, Tundra." Skye laughs, and waves that away. "He's kidding."

"No, he's not," I say, pegging Yarko with a look. "Best behavior with the ladies, got it?"

Yarko straightens and meets our gaze. "Got it."

"Got him!" Hawk shouts at the front entrance. "Yarko, are you here, buddy?"

We all jump up from the table and scramble to get to the front foyer.

"I'm here," Yarko says, jogging ahead of me. "Where do you need to be?"

While Hawk informs our young transport where we need to be, I take to the stairs and return to our guest suite. "Knock, knock. Does anybody want to wish us well? We're off to pull a goblin thorn out of our side."

"We found him?" Honor asks lighting up. She shuffles off the bed and hustles over to me. I try to keep my mind on the mission to come, but Honor hustling anywhere is a distraction.

How do women get anything done when they have such lovely body parts to jiggle?

"Why are you staring at my breasts?" Honor asks.

I lift my gaze and blink. "Sorry. I got distracted. Um...yes, Hawk says we've found him, and Lukas said you and Creed gave us the okay for lethal force."

Honor chuckles. "I more than give it, I encourage it."

"Consider it done." I open my arms and even though there's no real worry about rejection anymore, it makes my heart thump a little harder when she comes to me without hesitation. "We'll do you proud, Princess. I promise."

Her arms tighten around me, and she eases back, remaining

in my embrace. "I know you will. I just wish I was going with you."

"You are." Lukas comes in the door behind me, and we turn to greet him. "You're the Guardian of the Crown. It's your duty and purpose to be Dornte's champion, not mine. I was wrong to ask you to stay."

Honor steps back from our hug. "I don't think there's a wrong or a right. I'm the one with the ability to help him if something happens."

"But likely nothing will. He's been laying here for three hours since we found him. He might remain unconscious for another two days, we don't know. You have a destiny to fulfill. I'll stay with him. My magic might not be as on-point as yours is for this, but I've got game."

She flashes him a sexy grin. "Oh, I know you've got game."

He winks and gestures to me. "Go with Tundra and Dune, take out our bad guy, and get back here as soon as you can."

Honor studies his expression for a long moment and then dips her chin. "All right, we'll be back as soon as we can."

CHAPTER TWENTY-TWO

Honor

*L*ukas never ceases to surprise me. He's the one to think of the tracking method to find Ruic. He's the one who made that happen. And he's the one who stepped back so I can have my moment.

"Just when I think I can't love him any more than I do, he proves me wrong."

Calli smiles over at me as we get our boots on. "I always told Lukas I'd find him a mate worthy of his awesomeness. Despite his anxiety about the prospect, I think things worked out perfectly."

I chuckle. "Are you seriously taking credit for the two of us ending up together?"

"Hells, yeah because it was all me. If I wasn't with Hawk, Lukas wouldn't have been part of our entourage. And if that were the case, he wouldn't have been here when we followed Keyla into this realm, he wouldn't have helped us rescue you, and he wouldn't have sat with you for weeks, untangling the wicked web of magic the Blood Witch bound you with."

Crazy. That seems like forever ago.

"Fine. I'll give you the point. Although, I have a feeling he and I would've found our way to one another regardless."

"Destiny tends to work that way," Hawk says, checking his guns. "Is everybody ready?"

I glance around at our party. It's me, Tundra, Dune, Calli, and Hawk. Brant and Kotah aren't back from the Bastion yet. And Jaxx and Lukas are staying with Shadow.

Satellite imagery and heat signatures indicate the compound is deserted, so we're going in hard and fast before Ruic can arrange for more mercenary guards.

"Ready." I slide my palms against those of Tundra and Dune. When the five of us are linked up and holding hands, Yarko clamps Hawk's shoulder, and we transport.

The tingling surge of Yarko's power dances over my skin for a brief moment after we materialize at our destination. "Good luck, everyone," he whispers. "I'll be listening on comms. Call for me if you need an emergency evac."

He flashes out and then my adrenaline kicks in and I'm focused on the task at hand.

There's no need to stop and go over it again. Hawk laid it all out for us before we came.

Ruic's goblin gene signature was found inside this mountainside compound. The entire area is known to be fae saturated, so the risk of exposure from Dune and Tundra's presence is minimal.

While the people down the rocky slope might not know or recognize what an Elbirfae is, seeing them won't let any sacred fae cats out of the bag.

Hawk holds up his tablet and then points to the main house on the left with a stiff hand. Then, he points to his eyes and motions for Tundra and Dune to take tactical high points.

Tundra launches into the afternoon sky and settles on the

roof of the house. From his vantage point, he can see the compound and the courtyard.

Dune flies over to the lookout tower facing the slope of the hill we're perched upon. The steep incline drops sharply and overlooks a mountain town a mile below.

Technically, I should be the one in charge, but Hawk is both more aggressively alpha than I am and has decades more experience. I'm fine with me and mine following his lead for as long as I agree with the calls he's making.

I hope there never comes a point when we disagree because I don't look forward to locking horns with him.

"Ladies, you're with me," he whispers, checking the location on his tablet one last time before sliding it into his pocket.

"You're not trying to keep an eye on the girls to keep us safe, are you?" I ask, my need to clear the air on that rushing to the fore. "Neither Calli nor I need a big strong man to play the part of our hero."

Hawk looks back at me and chuckles. "No kidding. I'm the one who wants to stay safe. I don't have bulletproof feathers like your boys or inferno heat like Calli. I can't fight if I fly and can't fly if I'm shot. So, here we are."

Calli chuckles and pats a hand against his tactical vest. "Don't worry, hotness, we'll protect you."

The two of them resume studying the compound and I draw a deep, steadying breath. I'm so accustomed to proving myself I guess I misread that one.

Kudos to Hawk for his mindset.

The compound is a large stone monstrosity of a thing stuck on the side of a rocky mountain. A winding trail would allow for trucks with four-wheel drive to reach the pinnacle, but I suspect not many other vehicles would make it up here.

"How is Ruic Breard the only life sign we're tracking here?" I ask. "It's not like he has friends in this realm. He had to pay for mercenaries to fight for him at the Bastion."

Hawk frowns. "I only report the news. I don't write it."

"I appreciate that but it's odd that a place large enough for a hundred people has none…or one."

"Maybe he's squatting," Calli says. "Maybe he got a great deal on Airbnb."

Hawk shrugs. "This is your show, Honor. If you want to re-evaluate, that's your call."

I growl. "I want to storm the gates and take him down. I want this to be over so we can all get on with our lives. This asshole has skirted responsibility for every nasty and violent thing he's done. I want him to be put down."

I give Hawk credit.

In the minutes that follow, he doesn't try to rush me or make suggestions to sway my decision. He gives me a moment to go over what we know and what we think we know.

"Are we sure there's only one person here?" I ask.

Hawk shakes his head. "During an infiltration, there are no sure things. All we've got to go on is the intel we've been able to gather."

I stare at the compound and sigh. "It's like a staged show-room floor. Nothing out of place. Nothing to see. Nothing to warn us off. It feels wrong."

"And yet, Lukas's search says Ruic is here," Calli says. "Maybe he is here on his own. We ambushed his meeting at the Bastion. Maybe the get out of jail free teleportation spell he had was a one-way ticket and he just ended up here and is stranded."

"There are more questions every minute."

"Do you want to stand down?" Hawk asks, his voice level and calm.

My disappointment is so acute, it feels like a dagger is piercing my chest. "I don't. Lukas was so sure he'd find Ruic. I believe in him. I believe Ruic is here. I just…."

Calli glances around and frowns. "Maybe Lukas's worries

about Shadow distracted him. He's human. He might've made a miscalculation."

I think about that, and my gut says otherwise. "No. He was meticulous about the calculations. Even when the world is crashing around him, Lukas is as strong and sharp as always."

"More so, actually," Hawk says. "Lukas thrives under stress and adversity."

"Right. I believe in him and his abilities."

Hawk curses and glances around. "All right. So, what's our play here?"

I don't mean to be difficult. Dammit, if Lukas were here, he'd know exactly what to do. Maybe he should've come instead of me.

No. He was right. I am the Guardian of the Crown and it's my destiny to ensure my brother's kingdom remains safe. And the only way to do that is to take out scum like Ruic Breard.

"We're going in. I'm being stupid. Occam's Razor, right? The simplest answer is likely the right one. He's here. He's hiding. Let's go get him."

The three of us leave our cover, creeping along the stone wall of the building as we approach the entrance in single-file formation.

Hawk is on point and his guns are drawn and ready. Calli is in the middle, checking sightlines and scanning the compound. And I'm covering the rear, wings, and blaster out.

As we approach, I clear my mind, sweeping for any mental energy I can pick up.

Nothing.

No. It's not nothing…it's less than that.

It's almost a void.

The hair on the back of my neck stands on end and my skin rises in goosebumps. I double my efforts trying to figure out what I'm sensing.

We've almost reached the front door of the main building when I sense a surge of mental triumph and a rush of minds coming online.

Dozens of minds.

"It's an ambush," I say, panning my aim across the compound. "I feel them now. There must be a glamor hiding them from us."

"Well, fuck," Hawk says. "Then it's on."

Without any further discussion, Hawk stands and starts spraying bullets in a sweeping stream from in front of us, through the courtyard.

Calli ignites into her phoenix form and starts making a fiery sweep of the compound with her wings the same way Hawk is doing with his bullets.

The echo of gunfire and shouting bounces off the stone walls of the compound and hits us with a deafening force.

The glamor collapses and we're standing in the thick of it.

"Into the house," Hawk shouts, shoving me toward the door.

I stumble up the steps and fire my blaster. The locking mechanism melts, and I kick the wooden panel out of my way, scanning and aiming as we infiltrate the house.

Hawk comes in hard on my ass, slams the door shut, and then tips a large shelving rack from beside the door to block the entrance.

It's not lost on me that blocking the entrance of that mercenary fighting squad also means he blocked the exit for us.

That's a later problem.

Two men in black are running to intercept us and I launch into the air. Flying at them, I get my weapon up and take my shots. My setting is set to wide burst, and they fall without issue.

Landing at the junction of the main corridor, I search left, right, and forward for the next attack.

The shouts and screams outside are music to my ears.

Hawk's evaluation of our team was right. Calli, Dune, and Tundra are virtually indestructible. Ruic's hired guns likely didn't know what they'd be coming up against.

"This way," Hawk says, holding his tablet out.

Perfect.

If he's tracking our goblin, that's where we're going. There's no way I'm letting him use another teleportation spell to get away.

"This ends now, Ruic! Show yourself."

Glass smashes behind us but I don't have time to worry about that. There's enough trouble coming at us from the front.

The two of us rush through the building and it's maddening. After all the pain and turmoil, he caused to the citizens of Dornte, he's been hiding out in the lap of luxury?

Not fair.

Well, his lucky streak is about to change.

"On your left," Hawk shouts dropping right and raising his gun.

I push off the ground just as the bullets start flying. My flight takes me out of their reach but when I advance to take out our shooters, I catch something strung in the air.

The tripwire gives way just as I realize what the nearly inde-tectable line I've crossed is. The blast comes at me hard, fast, and head-on.

Blown back by the force of the explosion, I topple in the air head over feet in a spinning cartwheel until I hit a wall and drop to the floor.

"Move in. The female is down." I hear the voice in the distance, but it's sloshy in my head.

Fuck you. Okay, technically, I *am* down but pointing that out is just rude.

I can't stay down.

They're coming and I'm exposed.

I grunt, pressing my palms against the debris beneath me,

pushing myself up. My weapon was lost in the explosion but there are enough pieces of sharp and pointy things around, I can make do.

Pushing against my weight, I roll to get free of the debris. The air is thick with smoke, but I can't tell if it's the kind of smoke you get from a fire or just blowing up a section of a stone house.

Either way, my mouth is full of gravel, and it feels like the air is thick and gross in my lungs.

Gunfire close by gets my head back in the game.

I grab a chunk of pointy metal and grunt as I—*Well, shit*. I thought I was getting up.

Just kidding.

Not yet.

More gunfire. I'm pretty sure Hawk is keeping those mercs off me. I am forever grateful.

I make another attempt of getting to my feet and though it's not graceful, I manage to remain upright. When I list to the side, a strong arm wraps around my hips and keeps me from toppling.

Swinging the sharp piece of metal, I—

"Whoa, babe. It's me."

I blink at my tall, dark, and dangerous magic man and am thankful his reflexes are good. I would hate to have killed him. "Hey, what are you doing here?"

He blinks. "Later."

Right.

Lukas tucks me against his side and continues walking, firing his gun forward to clear our path. "Hawk?"

"Present," he says, shaking his head and joining us. "Got my bell rung by that explosion but retained all my parts and pieces."

"That's all that matters. Where are we headed?"

Hawk pulls out the tablet and the three of us start hiking down the hall.

"Tundra or Dune, I need one of you to make your way around the back of the main building," Lukas says. "There's a patio area with a narrow, winding stair down the side of the mountain. If we flush Ruic from his hiding place, ensure he doesn't get away on us."

CHAPTER TWENTY-THREE

Tundra

*L*ukas makes his request and I try not to laugh. Calli, Dune, and I are nipples-deep in hostiles, but sure, we can just clear this up and make our way to the back of the building. "We'll do our best," I say, trying not to sound belligerent.

"Tundra! Down!" Dune's command gives no room to wonder why. It's the kind of order that you obey without question.

Despite being locked in a hand-to-hand battle with two men, I drop to the stone ground and watch as a wall of flame consumes the heads and shoulders of my opponents.

They ignite like the heads of matchsticks, and I roll away from their manic flailing.

The searing heat of the fire is incredible. I draw my wing over my face and arms to keep my skin from bubbling and my lungs from singeing.

Calli is a fearsome ally, but her flames burn indiscriminately.

It doesn't matter that we're on the same side, if Dune hadn't warned me I would've been torched too.

With the two of them now out of the battle, I roll to my feet and check my surroundings. That's the last of the men on my side of the compound. There are a couple of stragglers jumping in a parked truck and honestly, if they want to bug out, I'm fine with that.

The engine of the utility truck rumbles to life and the tires squelch as the vehicle peels out. I guess they didn't sign up for a head-to-head with a fire-breathing mythical.

With that taken care of, I push off the ground, hover over the compound a moment to ensure the battle is won, and then pump my wings to carry me over the house.

Everything is as Lukas described. The back patio overlooks the town far below and there is a precarious staircase cut into the side of the mountain and winding down the side of the jagged stone.

It doesn't go all the way down, but it seems to lead to a cave in the mountain wall.

"In position," I say, flapping my wings to keep me hovering about thirty feet above the patio.

Dune joins me, does a bit of an aerial show, and smiles. "Yep. Tundra and I have your back door covered, magic man."

I cast Dune a sidelong glance. "Was that really necessary?"

He chuckles. "Like I told the kids, Warrior Lesson Number 2: battle can be grueling. Try to amuse yourself and your fellow warriors."

I shake my head. "Your so-called warrior lessons are not a thing. Stop saying they are."

Dune laughs. "Oh, they're a thing all right. And when I get the time, I'm going to lay out all the unspoken lessons that make a great Amberloq and call it the Amberloq Codex. Just wait. It'll be epic."

I roll my eyes and focus on the back of the house. "I'm terrified to admit it, but I'm sure it will be."

Lukas

Honor, Hawk, and I sweep through the back of the house as quickly and efficiently as we can while still testing for both explosive traps and glamors. If we've learned anything from this afternoon's battle is that what Ruic Breard lacks in courage, he tries to make up for in dirty tricks.

"Are you picking up anything?" I ask Honor leading the way through the last of the rooms.

"No. Nothing. But you've still got him on your screen, don't you, Hawk?"

"Yeah. Thirty feet ahead. He's either in a panic room behind that fireplace or there's another way into that space."

"Give me a second," I say, calling on a handy reveal spell that helps me see the unseen. The spell takes me only a moment to cast and the energy drain is minimal. "Yep. The bookshelf on the left has a hidden door and a passage to the space beyond."

"Did you hear that, Ruic?" Honor shouts louder than necessary. "We're coming for you, asshole."

I blink at the volume of her declaration, thankful that the only after-effects of Honor being blown up in an in-house bombing is that her hearing is shot for the moment.

I saw the detonation pattern of that blast. If she'd been on her feet when that hit, she would've been much worse off. The fact that she was airborne and blew back as far as she did before impact saved her from serious injury.

"Got it," Hawk says, stepping back from the bookcase. He raises his gun and uses his foot to slide the shelves out of the way. "We're coming in, asshole. Do me a favor and don't do anything stupid."

The second explosion of the night goes off and we're all grabbing for the closest wall to catch our balance.

"I think he did something stupid," I say, regaining my footing and rushing past Hawk.

"What did he say?" Honor shouts behind me.

I ignore the question, rushing through the narrow corridor that leads into the panic room. Debris is raining down from the ceiling and a large chunk of the exterior wall has been blown out.

A directional blast has given Ruic his escape door because other than the missing wall, the panic room is fully intact.

"Boys, do you have him?"

Two more explosions outside have me racing to catch up.

"You'd swear this fucker was a demolitions expert and not a currency maker," I say.

Two large clouds of smoke are still expanding in the air and dissipating.

"Boys, talk to me. Tell me you're all right."

"Yeah," Tundra says, coughing. "We'll be fine. He caught Dune's wing with one of his grenades and sent him spinning. I got to him before he impaled a wing on the rocks below, but it was close."

"Where did Breard go?"

"He's down there," Honor shouts, running to the edge of the balcony and diving over the side.

My heart beats hard at the base of my throat and I try to swallow past my coronary. I rush to the stone half-wall and look over the edge.

"Seriously, Honor. You are barely walking straight, can you not dive over cliffs?"

But, of course, my protests fall on deaf ears.

Racing to the edge of the balcony, I scan the narrow pathway below and find Honor flying a kamikaze attack straight at the fleeing male, her silver hair glistening in the sunlight. I've seen her fly a dozen times and her power is only matched by her grace.

That's not so today.

Her equilibrium must've been affected by the blast because she looks more like a drunk mosquito caught in the wind.

"Fuckety-fuck." Holstering my gun, I find the spot where the path begins its descent and—

Another explosion goes off.

"Honor!" my words rip at my vocal cords as I stare down at a cloud of smoke.

"I can't see. Was she hit? Where's Breard?" Hawk's frantic questions sound off beside me but I have no answers.

As fast as my feet can carry me, I'm navigating the narrow path. To say it's treacherous is generous.

It's a suicide path.

There's no choice...I have to get to her.

Glancing up every couple of seconds, I try to see what happened. Did Ruic take down Honor? Did Honor take down Ruic?

"Boys, can you see her? He detonated another one of those fucking grenades. Where is she?"

I'm three-quarters of the way down to the smoke cloud when I see her. She's sitting on the path on the other side of the detonation damage. She looks whole and alive.

My legs give out and I drop. My knees connect with the ground in a hard jolt, and I do my best not to fall off the narrow stone steps and to my death.

Fucking hell.

Hawk stops beside me and squeezes my shoulder. "I feel your pain, brother. My female does shit like this too."

I chuckle and try to get air into my lungs. "She's going to be the death of me."

Hawk laughs, hauling me to my feet. "Yeah, but she's the life in you too."

I suppose...but it's hard to see that at the moment.

"Pull up your big boy pants. Let's wrap this up and go home."

"Yeah, let's."

The two of us make our way down the next section of the mountain path and I find Honor catching her breath.

"Hey, babe, how are things?" I think it's more the movement of us arriving than my words that catch her attention.

"Hey, did you see? Our goblin took a tumble." She points down over the edge of the flimsy rope railing and chuckles. "You should have seen it live. It was amazing. He blew us both off the path, but I have wings and he doesn't. He made a couple of impressive bounces off rocks and then it was splat, splat, dead."

"Splat, splat, dead," Hawk says, grinning. "That has a lovely ring to it."

I wave that away and extend my hand to help her up. "I'm done with all this. Can we please go home?"

Honor gets to her feet and wraps her arms around me. "Hey, magic man," she shouts, much too loudly for the proximity of her mouth to my ear. "I'm tired of all this. Can we wrap this up and go home?"

I chuckle and give her a nod. "Yeah, great idea, babe. Let's do that."

Shadow

I wake to the slow and steady sawing of breaths and the knowledge that my mates are nearby. It's not so much a feeling as a truth my body and soul recognize. I feel them as tangibly as I feel my own body.

It's a comfort.

I lay there a moment more and the reality of my situation settles over me.

Damn. I remember grabbing one of the vials of tears from our restocking supply and swallowing them in the library. I was hoping I'd take them and start the healing process without anyone realizing I'd done it.

Then, once I saw what the healing properties of the tears did, I could explain to Lukas that everything was all right. Except I'm here now, lying in a bed, and by the ravenous twisting in my stomach, I've been out a long while.

Aside from my need for food, there is an even more urgent bodily calling prompting me to get up.

I tap the hip of the body beside me and the snoring stops.

"Shadow? Are you awake?"

The moment Lukas speaks, the timbre of his voice triggers something weird in my head. It's like a soft click. Like a light switch being flicked and then the world turns on.

I gasp as a brilliant glow silhouettes his body. "How is this possible? Did you give me something while I was out?"

"How is what possible? More words, Counselor."

I stare at the man I love and a warm rush spreads over my skin as excitement blooms. I don't want to move for the risk of breaking the spell, but nature calls. "I'm going to wet the bed if I don't get to the bathroom. Where are we? Where am I going?"

"We're in our suite. For the sake of expediency, I'll take you."

Good. That's good. "Yes, come with me. I don't want you out of my sight."

Lukas chuckles and I can't take my eyes off him. "You're acting weird."

"That's because I can see you...well, sort of. Mostly it's shapes and colors coming at me...outlines...maybe more like auras. Everything is lighting up around me...you, the furniture, the others. It's not me seeing exactly but I can make things out."

"That's wonderful, but how?"

"I don't know…it must be Calli's tears. It's like you're giving off a vibration or radiating energy. I see your aura."

Lukas has a hand under my elbow as he escorts me to the bathroom, but in truth, he doesn't need to. I can see the outline of the bathroom vanity and the shower and the toilet.

"I never thought I'd consider it a miracle to see that the lid of the toilet is closed, but I do." I reach down and lift the lid and the seat and proceed to empty my bladder.

Lukas is incredibly quiet behind me. That's fine. He's a man of strategic thought. He likes to observe and understand.

When I'm finished, I shake, tuck, and flush. I drop the seat for Honor and then go over to the sinks to wash up. I take extra time with the faucets, adjusting them, pump some soap, rinse, grab the hand towel.

Every little step is a triumph for me.

"Do all things give off energy?" I ask.

"I've never really thought about it," Lukas says. "I don't know. I would think all living things for sure, but I have no idea about plastics and glass or things like that."

"It doesn't really matter. The point is, I can see."

"You can what?" Honor's high-pitched excitement comes from the bedroom, but a moment later she's rushing through the bathroom door. "Did you say you can see?"

"Sort of. It's not sight like before it's…"

"It's true sight," Lukas says. "Or something close to it."

I stare at Honor with an intensity that makes my body tighten. Raising my fingers, I trace where her long, silver hair is brushing against her cheek. I follow the cascade down her collarbone, her shoulder, and down to the curve of her beautiful breasts.

Dropping to my knees, I gently cup her breasts in my hands and lean forward to give each of them a reverent kiss. "Hello, again my dear friends."

Honor giggles and runs her fingers into the back of my hair. "They say hello back."

"What's happening?" Dune asks, walking in with Tundra right behind him.

"Shadow is paying homage to Honor's breasts," Lukas says, chuckling. "Apparently, of all things, they are near the top of his list of things he missed when he lost his sight."

Dune nods. "Uh...yeah, that makes perfect sense. Those girlies are perfection."

Tundra chuckles. "I think you lost the lead in that, Dune. The point is that Shadow sees them."

"Yeah, that's awesome. I'm glad for you, my man, but it's three in the morning and if it's all the same, I'd rather celebrate with morning sex in like...five hours."

I laugh and nod. "Deal. Everyone back to bed. I didn't mean to wake you all."

"Nonsense," Lukas says. "You waking us up is perfection and the fact that you can see is even better. No apologies."

"Still, sleep is calling," Dune says.

"Yes, dear," Honor says, turning him back toward the bed. "Morning sex it is. Shadow's pick. He's the man of the hour."

Tundra follows them back to bed and I catch Lukas's wrist before he steps away. "I want to apologize."

He turns back to me and frowns. "I'm listening."

The playful joy of a moment ago dissolves and he crosses his arms over his muscled chest.

"I ignored your wishes regarding waiting with the tears and I'm sure when you found me, you were panicked and angry."

"Yep. You left out hurt."

I take the hit and nod. "I am sorry for the pain I caused you but I'm not sorry I drank the tears. Whatever control I've lost in my transition, I'm still a man, this is still my body, and I still get to decide a few things about how I want to live with what's happening to it."

"I wasn't trying to take your choices away from you, I only wanted to slow down and make educated decisions."

"And I appreciate that, but I couldn't stand to wait any longer. It's all on me. I cut you out of the decision-making process and I'm sorry. It won't happen again."

Lukas stares at me for a moment and then opens his arms.

My breath swells in my lungs and I accept the invitation. Meeting him chest-to-chest sets everything in my world right again. I turn my face into his neck and breath in his scent. "I love you."

Lukas kisses me with a gentle caress of his mouth and then eases back. "I love you too. And if you pull something like that again, I'm going to kick your ass."

"Understood."

My stomach lets off one hell of a growl and he chuckles. "How about we feed that beast and let Moonshade out for a bonus pee run before we go back to bed."

"That sounds perfect. I don't think I could sleep right now if I tried. I want to see everything."

Lukas laces his fingers with mine. "Maybe not everything, but at the very least, the Amberloq Hall kitchen. Come on. Let's get you something to eat."

CHAPTER TWENTY-FOUR

Honor

"I don't know what he was thinking, but he almost blew us both up." I reach for another homemade biscuit and break a piece off while I continue the recap for the Elbirfae at Valorous Hall. "We both blew off the winding path and into the air. It was only because I had wings and caught my fall that I lived."

"But he didn't," Clay says, satisfaction thick in the tone of his voice.

"No. Ruic Breard died a brutal and bloody death."

"Which is only fitting," Clover says.

"Splat, splat, dead," one of the kids says, chuckling. "That was my favorite part."

"Warrior Lesson Number 7," Dune says, holding up a finger as if he's about to impart sage wisdom. "Karma is real."

Tundra rolls his eyes and I fight not to laugh.

"We saw the media release of your return," Lark says, sitting on the arm of the couch. "Carrying him back to our realm in a body bag was an incredibly strong image."

Tundra nods. "We didn't arrange that, but it was good. It's good for citizens to know we'll go to any and all lengths to secure our realm and bring those who threaten the quadrant to justice."

"It'll certainly discourage those who think it's a good idea to challenge the Thornebane rule," Lark says. "There are also rumors that during the first battle with Ruic, someone challenged the Wolf King's rule."

Lukas waves that comment away. "That coup was snuffed out quickly. I doubt anyone will ever accuse Kotah of being weak again."

"Not unless they want their throat ripped out," Dune says.

Dozens of eyes widen around the room, but I'm not going to get into Kotah's story. These folks deserved to hear about Ruic Breard's takedown because they deserved closure.

Standing up, I pop the end of my biscuit into my mouth and wipe my fingers on my napkin. "And that's the end of that. We'll be here for another couple of hours. Tundra and Dune will need two volunteers to go to town for a grocery run. Shadow is set up in the study if anyone wants to talk to him about things you're troubled by or still processing. And Lukas and I are around if you have any other questions."

The gathering of the group breaks apart and they disperse. When the room clears, I notice Lark has made no effort to leave.

"Is there something I can do for you?" I ask.

"No, but there might be something I can do for you. Come with me. I'd like to get your opinion on something."

Lukas looks over at me and arches a brow.

I lift my shoulders in a shrug and follow her. Since our rather public confrontation regarding Elbirfae being allowed to move on, she's been nothing but respectful of our efforts to help them.

In fact, she's been integral to the recovery of the eighty people living here.

The two of us walk out to the main corridor and stop at the entrance. "That time you were here when you were searching in the library, Skye said you were looking for a private space where Valorous locked up discs or something?"

"The Guardian Chronicles, yes. Every female who holds my position is supposed to document their battles, triumphs, and losses to leave behind for the next generation. Since my aunt lived here instead of at Amberloq Hall, I hoped she kept up the tradition."

"But you didn't find them?"

"No. In our library, there is a little black mirror that acts as a DNA scanner. It is the key to unlocking my private library where the discs are held."

She launches straight up into the air, and I follow her. The two of us land on the fourth floor and strike off toward the Guardian's master suite. "It seemed inappropriate for any of us to move into this suite, but I've been searching the entire building for possible surprises left behind by the enemy."

She walks through the living space into the bedroom and hangs a left.

"And you found something in Valorous's walk-in closet?"

"When you said little black mirror...do you mean something like this?"

She sweeps a rail of clothing aside and gestures to a replica ID scanner to the one at Amberloq Hall.

"Yes, that's it! You found it." Racing over, I eye up the glossy, mirrored surface staring back at me. "Be kind to me, Valorous. Please let this work."

When I press my hand on the DNA scanner, I hold my breath for a couple of heartbeats until the soft *click* tells me we're in business.

"The one at Amberloq Hall is designed to only allow access to the female Thornebane. I assume this one would be the same."

In my library, triggering the security check-in releases a hidden compartment to access the vault behind the wall. In this closet, I have no doubt I know where both of those things are.

"This is the same as our private panels in our suites in the castle." I press on the wall panel and shift it out of the way. Instead of a safe, like in my closet in the Heirs' Suite in the castle, this private panel exposes an opening into a chamber beyond.

Stale air rushes out to greet me and my entire body is consumed with goosebumps.

Valorous didn't forget me.

I find the light switch on the wall to my right and step inside. The cabinet on the far wall is filled with rows and rows of jade tablets the same as the ones in my library at home.

I consider plugging a few into the console but discard the idea almost as quickly. This isn't my Guardian Library. I'll take these discs home with me and watch them there.

Turning back to the entrance of the room I call out, "Lark, could you get me a cardboard box or something to pack these discs up, please?"

"Of course. I'll be right back."

While she's gone, I take a look at the runes she used to mark them. Oh, thank goodness, Valorous dated them. That will make transporting them and putting them back in order so much easier.

Running my finger across the runes and pictographs that describe the topic of the disc, hope blooms that these will be the last pieces for me to put together my Guardian of the Crown puzzle.

I suppose I need to create a disc of my own.

After all, my guardians and I squashed the rebellion, instated a new, global currency for the realm, and conducted the first joint realm manhunt to catch our fugitive. That's got to be disc worthy.

Lark returns and stops at the doorway, holding out a box. "I'd come in and help, but I'm getting the sickening feeling this room doesn't like me."

I chuckle. "Don't be offended. I think it was designed not to like anyone but me."

Setting the box on the desk, I notice a disc still sitting in the console. My heart aches. That's the last Chronicle disc she ever watched before her death.

Or maybe not...

It could also be the last Chronicle disc she ever recorded. What if, during the siege on the compound, when the Blood Witch was poisoning her people, she came in here to tell me something?

A rush of energy sweeps through the room, and the hair on the nape of my neck stands on end.

I slide behind the desk and blow the dust off the console. Placing my thumb on the activation pad, the disc activates and my blood rushes from my head.

The wall opposite the desk lights up and my aunt appears in the projected image. "Well done, little warrior," she says, calling me by her pet name for me. "If you're watching this, I'm dead and you've been left scrambling."

"Yep. Pretty much," I say to the screen.

"I'm sorry. I'll carry that sorrow with me to my grave. There are so many things I hoped to teach you. I'm ashamed to say your father and I wasted too much time being stubborn and angry with one another to make that happen. Tell him I regret that most of all."

"I would, but he's dead too." A part of me hopes she found him in the afterlife and told him herself.

"I'm proud of you for finding your way here, little warrior. By now, if any of us live, your Biome Generals have activated and come to aid you. Embrace their help. It is not a sign of weakness to admit you need help, it's a sign of true strength."

"I didn't have much of a choice, but yeah, we managed all right in the end."

"As much as I hope this disc is a precaution, if you're watching me now, it's not. There's a plot in motion to take over your father's throne. In the past weeks, there were whispers of treachery, caches of money moved, and a dozen of my scouts killed. I called my force home to ready for battle but played into the hands of the enemy. We've been trapped. All Amberloq will die with me."

"Except for the two you sent for a time-out on a mountaintop. You neglected to recall them." I'm not actually angry about that. If she'd called Tundra and Dune back to service, they'd be dead too.

Everything works out as it is meant.

"The most important thing you need to know, and won't find in any of the discs, is that I've been working on developing a new breed of Amberloq Warrior—a genetically engineered super-soldier."

I blink at the screen. "What the fuckety fuck?"

"Your father was against it from the start and inevitably, it drove us apart. He thought I was playing god, but protecting Dornte and in extension, the entire realm, is my destiny and my honor."

"I get that, but genetically engineered soldiers? I think I'll side with my father on this one. It sounds like a dangerous prospect."

"You'll find the compound in a remote part of the Dornte Fringe near the foothills. Talk to Remi at the Gauntlet and she'll help you find it. The program is being overseen by Andras Brass. He'll fill you in on everything we've achieved."

She stops talking and sighs at the screen. "I'm sorry, Honor. I wish things had been different. Hopefully, you find what you need in the discs I've left for you. I truly wanted to be a better mentor than destiny allowed me to be. I believe in you, little warrior, and always have, even if I wasn't there to tell you."

When the projection stops and the image ends, I stare at the room and try to process.

Holy hell. Super-soldiers?

Lukas

Honor returns to the Great Room with a box in her arms and a million emotions flittering across her face. I jump up and meet her in the doorway. "What is it, babe? What's happened?"

"Super-soldiers," she whispers, shock and confusion warring in her expression. "That's what the rift was about between Valorous and my father. She's got some kind of *Universal Soldier* project in the Fringe...or, at least, she did before she was killed."

I take the box from her arms and set it on the floor by the door. Moonshade bounds over to see what I've got and sniffs the contents.

Straightening, I pull Honor to the side to keep our convo private. "Before she was killed...that was more than two years ago. Wouldn't a squad of super-soldiers have surfaced by now?"

"Apparently not. Maybe? Honestly, I have no idea. All I know is she told me to go to the Fringe, track down the guy in charge, and get caught up on the project she dedicated her career to."

"That's not overwhelming at all."

"I know, right?"

Dune, Tundra, and Shadow join us, and we get them caught up on what happened with Valorous.

"What the hell does that mean?" Dune asks. "And why wouldn't we know about that? She kept it a secret even from us? I'm hurt."

I chuckle. "Seriously? Weren't you the problem child? Are

you really surprised she didn't confess her super-secret life-long mission to you?"

Dune makes a face. "Are you trying to cheer me up, magic man, because if you are...you suck at it."

Honor laughs and pats Dune's chest. "I have no idea what her motivation was or why she did any of the things she did, sweetie. All I know is what she said in the video."

Tundra frowns and picks up the box. "Well, whatever her reasoning, it's done, and we've inherited the responsibility. It looks like we've got our next Amberloq mission laid out for us."

Shadow wraps an arm around the small of her back and gives her a squeeze. "Whatever comes at us, we've got you, Princess."

Damn, it does my heart good to see how Shadow has bounced back. Calli's tears couldn't erase him being an Oracle, but even Demarco thinks the worst is behind us.

We have a long and exciting future ahead of us, I'm sure of it. "I say, we head home, take our dinner up to our suite, and brainstorm our next steps."

Honor looks at me and laughs. "Brainstorm, eh? Is that what the kids are calling it now."

Tundra, Dune, and Shadow all get a kick out of that one.

"Well sure, there can be other activities to free the mind after we fuel up."

"Check please," Dune says raising his hand. "Yo, Yarko, time to take the adults home."

Yarko and Skye jog out of the recreation room laughing. "No problem."

"Do we *all* have to go now?" Skye asks. "We're in the middle of a crazy game Terran made up. I think I might be winning. It's too convoluted to tell."

Tundra thinks about that and shakes his head. "No. Yarko can bring you all back when you're finished. Don't stay out too late. Maybe...nine o'clock?"

Dune snorts and the rest of us don't do much better at keeping our amusement to ourselves.

Tundra glares at us and frowns. "What? I thought that was being lax and lenient."

Skye giggles and gives him a quick pat on the arm. "It's super cute you thought so. 'Kay, see you later."

Skye runs off and Tundra adjusts his hold on the box and looks at Yarko. "What does that mean? Is she planning on coming home at nine or not?"

Yarko looks torn. "I don't think so."

"Eleven is fine," I say, reaching forward so Yarko can transport us home. "And not a minute later."

Yarko gives me a firm nod. "Got it. I'll make sure."

Tundra frowns. "That's late. She's only sixteen."

I see his point and make an amendment. "You don't leave here, and you come straight home. No side trips or your privileges will be reassessed."

"He gets it," Honor says, laughing at us. "Home please, Yarko. I'm looking forward to refueling and a few hours of brainstorming with my mates."

Yeah baby. "Sounds like a plan."

ENDNOTE

Thank you for reading – **Honor Empowered.** While the story is fresh in your mind, and as a favor to me, please leave a review and tell other readers what you thought.
A quick star rating and/or even one sentence can mean so much to readers deciding whether or not to try a book, series, or a new-to-them author.
Thank you.
And if you loved it, continue with the Guardians of the Fae Realms with book 13 in the series and Lark's harem. **Find the Fallen.**

Author Notes

Written on 21/03/2022

I hope you enjoyed **Honor Empowered,** book 12 of the Guardians of the Fae Realms, and getting to know Honor, Lukas, Shadow, Tundra, and Dune.

I have two more trilogies planned for this series. Next up is for Lark to find her place as an Amberloq Biome General in **Find the Fallen.**

I'm looking forward to writing Lark's story, but first, I have another series I'm relaunching that I'll be spending my JL writing time on until the summer.

Exemplar hall was originally released as a 5-book Urban Fantasy Academy series in 2019. Now, with the popularity of Zodiac Academy, my co-author and I are dusting it off and RH-ing the hell out of it for a relaunch.

Captured by the Magi is book one and features the same story, just with a deepening of the relationships and the addition of fated mates, enemies to lover, and best friend tropes. The betas gave it two thumbs up and we're thrilled.

Hugs to all,

JL

Find Me

My Direct Sales Site: Shopify
My books
Web page – www.jlmadore.com
Email – jlmadorewrites@gmail.com
Newsletter – JL Series Updates

Find the Fallen

Guardians of the Fae Realms: an action-packed Fae Romance series by International Bestselling Author JL Madore!

The wars are over and it's time to rebuild the quadrant of Dornte.

When Lark is tasked to locate and rescue a **missing group of super soldiers**, the dangers of their dark past threaten the fragile peace of the quadrant. As the newest and first ever female Biome General, **she can't allow that to happen.**

Connor senses the violence brewing in Lark and while he knows how to **soothe her savage beast with his own**, it's only a temporary solution. The draw she feels to the fallen warriors is not only undeniable but it's growing...and so is his.

From the moment Lark and Connor meet the Fallen their fates are sealed.

Captured by the Magi

An action-packed fantasy romance series from International Bestselling author JL Madore and debut author Ruby Night!

They came for my twin and left me behind because women hold no power in the magi world.

They're about to find out how wrong they are...

Jesse Storme. Bartender. Rock-climber. And the girl left behind.

One minute, Wyatt and I are scaling our favorite rock peak and enjoying a moment of escape from our crappy lives. The next, **we're attacked, and my brother is gone.**

I think it's connected to the creepy recruiter dude from **Exemplar Hall.**

I find out it's so much worse than that...

Sucked into a **Hunger Games meets Harry Potter** event to rescue him, I don't know who I can trust. I'm a girl posing as a guy. I'm not supposed to be here. And I'm definitely not supposed to have the power I do.

Doesn't matter. I would suffer any pain to find and save Wyatt.

*We're more that twins—***We're Gemini Twins.**

ALSO BY JL MADORE

Book 1 – Captured by the Magi

Book 2 – Jesse and the Magi Vault

Book 3 – The Makings of a Magi Knight

Book 4 – Clash with the Magi Council

Book 5 – The Unstoppable Storme

Club Sanguine

Book 1 – Moonstone Maelstrom

Book 2 - Sunstone Sacrifice

JL's More Traditional M/F, M/M, or Menage

The Watchers of the Gray Series (Paranormal)

Book 1 – Watcher Untethered – Zander

Book 2 – Watcher Redeemed – Kyrian

Book 3 – Watcher Reborn – Danel

Book 4 – Watcher Divided – Phoenix

Book 5 – Watcher United – Seth

Book 6 – Watcher Compelled – Bo

Book 7 – Watcher Unfeigned – Brennus

Book 8 – Watcher Exposed – Taharqa

The Scourge Survivor Series (Fantasy)

Book 1 – Blaze Ignites

Book 2 – Ursa Unearthed

Book 3 – Torrent of Tears

Book 4 – Blind Spirit

Book 5 – Fate's Journey

Book 6 – Savage Love – epilogue novella

Aliens of Atlantis Series (Sci-Fi)

Book 1 – Taryn's Tiderider

Book 2 – Kai's Captive

Book 3 – Alyandra's Shadow

www.ingramcontent.com/pod-product-compliance
Lightning Source LLC
Chambersburg PA
CBHW050425260626
47156CB00003B/1158